TALL DEAD

TALL DEAD WIVES

ROWLAND MORGAN

BLOOMSBURY

First published in Great Britain 1990

10 9 8 7 6 5 4 3 2 1

Copyright © 1990 Rowland Morgan

The moral right of the author has been asserted

Bloomsbury Publishing Limited, 2 Soho Square, London W1V 5DE

A CIP catalogue record for this book is available
from the British Library

ISBN 0 7475 0721 X

Photoset by Rowland Phototypesetting Limited,
Bury St Edmunds, Suffolk

Printed and bound in Great Britain by
Richard Clay Limited, Bungay, Suffolk

**FOR MARK HOWELL
AND TOM SHANDEL**

Poor in troubles . . .
Poor in dreams.

Chinese Proverb

PART ONE

JOINED IN HOLY

1

IT was a lilikoi flower that took me into the hills. After ten days in the islands I'd hit a muggy spell, and Hans Regner, one of the founders of Hawaiian botany, had mentioned a spot above Kahuku Point where he said I could find a rare purple variety of the passion flower: *passiflora edulis* Sims, or lilikoi.

A few hundred feet up, where the stifling haze of the beach gave way to a raspberry-flavoured breeze, I stopped and got out of my rentawreck Cutlass convertible. From the northeastern tip of Oahu it was thirteen hundred miles of empty ocean to my home near Santa Flora on the California coast. Right behind my villa on the beach was the grave of Laurie Wallace, a grassy mound with a simple wooden crucifix.

I thought of Laurie, how ocean scenery got to her. How we'd explored San Mateo county for alfresco sex. An amazing session in a valley on the coast had made her buy the waterfront half-section there. Perhaps she'd sensed she was dying.

Then she was dead, and the designs for Valle Verdosa made my name. Cody Wallace was Mister Co-op, Mister Conservatory-kitchen, Mister What-the-heck-does-*that*-look-like? of the Year. I'd sold everything but the house and her resting place in the back forty and never drawn another elevation. It became: Whatever Happened to Cody Wallace? Which I preferred.

A tarry ribbon wandered up the flank of the island to a headland with two white pods built on it. One was a domed cylinder with a sprig of aerials, the other taller and bulb-tipped, a sixty-foot penis with a world-beating glans. I parked on a gravel apron outside the compound to admire these exercises in raw function. Whatever communications hoohah went on inside them, the look of the buildings shouted something refreshingly primitive back at sea and sky. A lover felt a kinship.

Peppi had taken one of her Olympic dips, halfway to Borneo and back. My idea was to be waiting with a bunch of *passiflora* when she emerged. First, to find them.

As Hans had instructed, a sign indicating the Waialua Scout Camp was fixed onto a padlocked gate, which I climbed over. Past the paddocks, the trail kept climbing, up a scrubland valley towards the spine of the Koolau range, arid country, but Hans had said to look nearer the camp so I hiked on.

After Laurie there'd been no one. Four years of no one. The imprint of her had remained on my skin. Her shade had lingered, gently chiding and teasing. Until gradually, not long ago, the voice had faded and her presence had slipped away, leaving me listless, out of tune. After I'd tried everything else, my friends and neighbours had persuaded me to take a holiday that I'd justified with some research at the Bishop Museum.

At the neck of the valley the lane forked. A double finger post pointed one way to the camp, the other to the riding stables. I took the camp route and wandered along examining the scrawny slopes for purple blossoms. Apparently they grew on a kind of ivy, but I had only a tenuous, jet-lagged idea of whether the season was right. At least it was warm. Thoughts of Laurie gave way to dreams of honeymoons.

After a mile or so I noticed a dust plume in the distance, first sign of life in the foothills. In a while two pint-size riders in dusty T-shirts and jeans were approaching on go-bikes. Their size played tricks with scale, so that they still seemed a fair way off when they hauled up twenty paces away, pygmies caked in wholewheat flour, shouting: 'Go back!' as they shattered the peace with their lawn-mower engines, glaring at me through grimy facial slits.

'Take it easy, guys,' I said, making the three-fingered salute and thinking how standards had declined in the Boy Scout movement.

'You'll see!' the wild tykes shouted back, U-turning away with their mini-engines snorting.

I walked on in their tracks, toying with the idea of coming back another day for the lilikoi, when I spotted the crimson glory of a pair of 'apapane birds in shrubs ahead and forgot about the little intrusion.

That was when the pickup truck bobbed up over a rise fifty yards ahead, giving off waves of nastiness.

It was an old cod-faced short-box 50s Ford, and three hairy outriders were straphanging from the mirror brackets like baboons. I went and stood on the verge, waiting for it to pass, but the outfit scrunched to a halt in my path.

The head honcho slithered down out of the driving seat and approached, leaving his supercharged engine grumbling. His jean suit was torn and stained, the pointy Texan boots were silver-tipped and pigeon-toed, and the fencing-shirt collar was turned up around a bunch of gleaming black curls. A brass death's-head dangled from his left earlobe, and the rest of his face, of the breed known as craggy, was twisted with primitive emotions which backlit the eyes propane-torch blue and set his teeth grinding.

He trespassed into my space and stood flexing his hands as if he was going to heft the planet. His speech came in a groan of pain.

'Gedoffa this freakin' lan' y'freakin' asshole. Whut th'fut y'think y'doin'? Futt'n asshole!'

An image of Peppi came to me: emerging from the turquoise sea, surging up on glistening honey-coloured thighs, with streaming golden seaweed hair. Incoherent jealousy stabbed my gut, curdling the juice of crazy love I'd felt there into bitter apprehension. Einstein matched me pound for pound but there was the help watching. And the coolest, most restrictive factor was the array of heavy-gauge carbines racked against the back window of the pickup's cab.

I was carrying an Instamatic. My outfit was huarachos, cut-off jeans and an antique Hawaiian shirt with a ballpoint in the breast pocket. Leering and shrugging like a dimwitted tourist stray, I said: 'Why, I'll turn right round and hike on back home if I'm both'rin' you folks any.'

By way of reply Einstein socked a broad palm against my chest so that I collapsed on my coccyx, which hurt. The ape committee looked on, ready to take notes, as their president demonstrated how to swing a steel-tipped boot at a head.

Panicking, I rolled with it and got away with a graze.

'Now, *brother*!' I protested, scrambling to my feet genuinely aghast. 'Exactly what is your beef? You could've broke my Kodak.' I pored over my camera, getting a grip on the carrying thong. It made a kind of flail, and I swung it desperately at the ringleted brow.

He fended it off easily with a forearm, the camera went flying and the head jerked back, giving me a glimpse of an ill-shaven windpipe, which I pincered at arm's length with surgical ferocity, feeling the gristly tube crunch under my fingers. His face went puce and he uttered a raven's croak before chopping my wrists away, gasping.

Which exposed the side of his neck, so I whipped out my ballpoint in a fist and pounded it ink first at the sternomastoids just above the collarbone. It failed to penetrate the jean cloth, so as his skull came round I nutted it near the frontal/sphenoid joint. There was a 'toc' as our crania hit. He bellowed and barged me down. I tried to pull him with me but he swung one of the glinting boots towards my groin, so my fists went there protectively instead and I hit the ground groaning and hawking, rolled up in a foetal ball of Method agony.

Einstein gave me a good review. He grunted, dusted me off his palms, raked back his tresses, climbed back into the truck muttering about assholes, and made like a tiger with his engine. The outfit accelerated by, leaving the trail defiled with a smell of hair oil, and my fallen body, gathering dust.

Shaken, suddenly profoundly confused about Hawaiian aloha and oblivious of highland flora, I retrieved my pen and camera and walked back between fresh tire tracks, worrying about whether the go-bike brats had slashed my upholstery or stood on a fruit box and taken a leak in the fuel tank.

It was a long way without honeymoons.

When I got there the engine started, so I put it into Drive – but quickly pushed it back to Park and peered out into the undergrowth. There was hairy ivy trailing down the fence a few yards away and a solitary mauve blossom was hanging on it, extravagantly petalled with a kind of rotor arm at the centre. A purple lilikoi, no mistake. I got out and plucked it, laid it on the seat beside me and drove hard towards Waimea Bay, a white-wine spritzer and a gazelle of a lifeguard.

Armed with my rare flower, I dismissed the jerk in the pickup with a shrug as a dope farmer paranoid about his crop.

I had it wrong.

2

SAL, bartender at the Pooka Shell on Waimea Bay, looked like one of Fletcher Christian's mutineers after three weeks in an open boat: bleached hair, scrawny beard, long bony limbs, Slavic cheekbones and penetrating stare. It was a local tradition he alone kept up. When I came in, he was as usual working a couple of topless truants, giving them a cut price on returnable Cokes with free straws.

'American female'll be obliged to study the human dick in high school soon, y'know that?' he said, fixing them with the slightly walleyed bomb craters, making them exchange get-him looks, rolling their eyes.

I leaned on the zinc top, smoothing an ice cube on my forehead and checking the view. The lifeguard chair, set on a six-foot frame, stood empty.

Sal breathed on a beer glass, gave it a final hone with a Map-of-the-Philippines dishcloth and placed it on the mirrored shelf behind the bar.

'Yep,' he said. 'This chick I know is into theosophy, man.'

'Uh-huh,' the girls went.

'Goes to lectures by this Rudolf Steinbagel guy on the nature of the hard on.'

'Steinbagel, huh! Zattafact.'

'Mystery of the phallus. In Honolulu, first Thursday each month. She's ahead a her time.'

'Uh, what's the mystery, Sal?'

'Impotence, baby!' he proclaimed with a prophetic sweep of the free hand. 'Preshoot! One-minute milers! They ravaging the enn-tire western world. They's barely one stand-up, shake-it-out, sixty-minute man left in any of our major metropolises. Surveys prove.' He brought a glass up to the light, squinted through it and placed it on the shelf.

'Shee-it,' one of the beachkids groaned.

'Let me tell you, it is *the* fee-male thrower of the 1990s,' Sal insisted, poking another glass at them with the cloth plugged into it. ''Cos you all got t'get married again now. You got t'be raised under lock 'n' key and traded off the first time you see the light a day outside. Anybody who ain't married's a whore then, better believe it. Branded on the tit and confined to an institution.'

The girls gaped and broke up. Sal was way better than Socials.

I put the ice cube down and fingered saliva onto the graze on my temple. The guy was a child of the brief era of free love, he wanted to talk the future off. Tropical seasons had slipped by and left him, only a decade out of high school, a kindly peculiarity, like the Pooka Shell, maintained by the county of Honolulu out of sentimentality and neglect. From outside, the place looked like a prop from *Gilligan's Island*, or 'The Road to Mandalay'. The make-believe thatch roof was composed of pink plastic raffia bleached white by sun and surf, and the plywood walls with their shuttered windows were held together by layers of concert posters. Inside, the wall behind the bar was papered with a faded blow-up photograph of Waikiki Beach in the 1880s. Its virgin sands and coconut groves were as empty as the Pooka Shell on an out-of-season weekday.

My neck hair bristled. The lifeguard was on the high chair thirty yards away, watching the crescent-shaped beach of Waimea Bay. Thunderheads were unfurling beyond her in the northwest over Kauai. A breeze lifted the crinkly papaya-coloured hair. Waves made war-drum music for the enthroned figure, sitting elegantly poised and staring out at an iron-hard horizon.

Hard to stroll up to someone propped in the air like that and pass the time of day. I sighed and pushed my glass forward. The spritzer Sal poured picked up the golden highlights on the hair

9

I loved. He uncapped a couple of Colas and stood them in front
of the girls.

'Aw heck,' he said. 'Who knows what the hell's goin' on with
sex any more, anyhow?'

I echoed: 'Indeed,' but reflected: Sal should. The quaintness
of his laughing blue-gray eyes and speed-freak stoop gave him
the air of an eccentric hobo far beyond his years, and the beach
bunnies made an airport lounge out of his cottage a mile along
the beach.

The spring water and Napa Valley riesling washed through
my fresh-kicked head like innocence. Out the dusty window the
lifeguard leaned forward, swung round, climbed perfectly down
the rungs of the chair and strode away towards the flat-roofed
beach office flanked by its stacks of folded canvas recliners. I
watched the stately figure move, like a tribal Masai balancing a
water jar, into the interior darkness.

'Y'know sex appeal is just 'bout dead?' Sal started up again.

'Uh-huh?' the girls went, simultaneously sloping Coke bottles
against sixteen-year-old pouts.

The lifeguard was re-emerging into the sun with a straw hat
on.

'Take the commercials!' Sal said. 'Tampax, Kotex, pussy
sprays, rubbers, make-up, deodorant, underwear, toilet cleaners,
blood-sucking detergents, mattresses, candlelight dinners, bank
loans, rubbers, Aids – the thrill is gone, babe, y'know what I
mean?'

'No respect, right?' a girl's voice said archly.

'Right. Your average sisterhood hauls and mauls on a wang
like it's nothin' more'n a teat on a cow. It's no wonder there's a
major lack of blue-veiners in the land.'

They spluttered and chortled. Sal knew how.

The brim of the unwise hat bent back in the breeze.

'Sex is dead,' Sal announced, poking his cloth into a glass
and rubbing it out.

'That depends, Sal,' I muttered.

She had to keep looking out to sea. More people were floating
on boards off the point than were making use of the beach, which
was about empty. The surfers were specks, paddling aimlessly
around against the stormy backdrop, waiting for the right crest.

Occasionally a bunch of them climbed up and ski-rode a roller in towards the rocks, then it was paddle-paddle all the way out again.

The hat came off and I won a private bet.

''Course it's cleanest if there's no contact,' Sal went on. 'No mind games, no word manipulations. Yer unconscious powers by-passin' the ego and communicatin' directly with yer chakras. You can be standin' there rappin' 'bout different types of crystal and what they do, real polite, clothes on 'n' everythin', when what's really happenin' is a breeder reactor behind the guy's balls is lightin' up a sign inside the sister's pelvis, sayin' *spread*.'

Sal grinned, they grinned, and I marvelled absently at how the routine worked. I needed one.

The lifeguard was climbing down off the chair, forwards this time, with a nifty twist of the hands and a thrust-out belly. She was so ta-a-all . . .

'Hey, Cody,' Sal called down the zinc. 'You bin eyeballin' Peppi all week. When you goin' to make yer move?'

My breeder reacted lushly through the shanty wall, across the sand and up against her perfect behind as she ran for the bowling straw disc of her hat. The power illuminated inside her a flowing copperplate sign like something off the marquee of a Las Vegas hotel, which revolved in a velvety night of the unconscious, flashing *love*, blink, *love*, blink, *love*.

She kept going.

I grabbed my glass and followed.

3

PEPPI chased her hat out of sight. I lay down on the sand with my spritzer and waited, not clear on how to make an approach, but hopeful that true love would find a way. Hope had been thin soup all week.

The air smelt pinkly of papaya skin and ozone, gusting about restlessly. The muggy sky was getting overcast, but I'd been out in Hawaiian showers before, enjoyed the way the Pacific swell rolled in and pounded the hell out of Oahu, and the way Oahu got her own back by using jagged mountains to gut the clouds. The idlers on the beach would head for their cars, close the roof and smoke the Big Island's potent sensemilla, but I liked to make a bundle of my book, towel and wallet, tuck it under my head and get wet.

Soon the sky was distracting me from Peppi. It turned into purple cauliflowers and swirled and brimmed and expanded like a tape on fast forward, filling the view with black-and-blue whorls. Sand started machine-gunning my windward flank, and the palm trees on the point bowed down and blew out like burst umbrellas. The ocean surface went flat and rocked, with spume skidding and swirling over it. Something orange caught my eye: it was a tent from the camp site, ballooning overhead, gaining height fast. A yellow one kited after it. This was no shower.

A gust as solid as a river rolled me over and smacked my face in the grit. I clung to planet Earth.

It cost me a facial sandblasting to pick out the hazy form of the barroom through a whistling haze of dust and detritus. There was no question of standing up, I had to settle for scrambling along on my belly in the dust like Eve.

When I got to the bar it was shuttered up and I pounded on collectible Camel, Winston and Lucky plates until the door opened a crack and a long gangly arm with a knuckly hand at the end of it clasped my nostalgia shirt collar and yanked, tearing it half off.

Inside you could see it was empty, but you still couldn't hear.

'Make it a Gridlock,' I shouted, and Sal padded back to the bottles to shake up his cocktail of lime, brandy, cinnamon, vanilla, green chartreuse and soda.

I looked round, not surprised that the girls had fled, because the Pooka in a kona gale made a lousy fraid-hole. The thatched bar canopy was doing a straw hula dance. Creaking noises in the rafters accompanied every surge of the storm, and the plywood walls bulged with each roar of the big bad wolf outside.

I crossed the room to the bar, took hold of cool zinc and put a foot on the rail. There was a crash, the door broke open and my lifeguard swept in with the gale. Sal raced to repair the latch behind her and she stood astride the middle of the dance floor laughing and shaking the grit off the front of her T-shirt.

She glowed like an ikon of human reproduction. Each time the wet cotton slapped against her chest the Zs in the rubric ZZ TOP there made a pair of humps like longboat prows. A scanty triangle of orange fabric swelled below her taut belly, and the bare legs were king-size Longs made for leaping out of raiding vessels to bash yokels on the head. Apricot hair radiated from her scalp in electric crinkles, and her smile irradiated the place like a stove.

I broke out of her spell and turned to my cocktail.

'Sal, you reveal heroic qualities. Why there's even a little green Chinese umbrella.'

'And a price of four dollars seventy-five.'

'In this?'

He put down the roll of wire he'd used on the door, churned the cash register, which was inaudible, tore off a tab and placed it in front of my glass which, not to be outdone, I drained and dabbed forward for a refill. What the hell, if we'd been at sea our ship would have been doing neck flips.

A silvery voice powered by a trained diaphragm cut through the gale behind me: '*Poor naked wretches, wheresoe'er you are, that bide the pelting of this pitiless storm, how shall your houseless heads and unfed sides, your loop'd and window'd raggedness –* '

It broke off and I looked round. She beamed at me, scratched one of her breasts, and spat accurately on the deck, using a technique that made a gun barrel out of her tongue. The dab of clear gob whacked onto the bare boards near my feet.

'Sand in my teeth,' she announced.

'But you got the hat,' I blurted.

She winked, threw the hat aside and doggy-shook her head, making her hair wheel out and spray the room. Then she froze the movement, looking a fraction of an inch past my eyes as the hair slapped her face.

'Lime juice cocktail suit you?' I called, scuffing some of the sand off my grazed cheek and projecting across a roar worse than a touchdown in injury time.

She nodded, crossed hands and pulled off her T-shirt, releasing the rose-tipped jugs in bouncing joy. Then she hooked her thumbs into the cords at her hips, stepped out of the monokini and wrung it out on the floor. Her all-over tan seemed to fight off the storm.

'*Blow wind, and crack your cheeks!*' she bellowed with theatrical force, chuckling as she wrung out the T-shirt.

It would have been insulting to the Great Creator to look away. I gave the drink signal to Sal, who was ready with the shaker.

Peppi scratched her tawny beaver, stepped the extra-longs back into her G-string, yanked it up with a pelvic wriggle, hauled on the wrinkled T-shirt and approached the bar, declaiming some more: '*Is there no balm in Gilead? Is there no physi –* '

Whoo-oo – *crash!*

With a yowl of protest the typhoon heaved the barroom wall at us. I sprang forward and hunkered with my arms round Peppi like a farm boy grabbing a sack of grain, and she came down on top of me in a heap of barrier-cream scent and damp hair.

The wall and part of the roof followed us a microsecond later, and the spars which would have cracked her head open hit the chrome mushroom stools instead.

I lay keeping the embrace tight, with her pubic bone grinding on my thigh in a parody of desire. There was a seething maelstrom swirling overhead. And two rusty nails were suspended from a beam six inches off the nape of her neck.

It didn't last long. Whimsical and easily bored, the storm abruptly dropped us and wandered away in search of another island to play with, and a cowboy whoop cut the silence, coming from under the heap of splintered timbers which had been a bar.

4

I LAY beneath the lifeguard I loved savouring a mouthful of hair. When she shifted, rotten wood chips and termite husks fell. We clambered out of the wreckage into steaming sunshine. The show was back in Polynesian Technicolor.

Chunks of roofing had to be cleared to get at Sal and he climbed out clasping a quart of Cutty Sark, which got him a ragged cheer from the bathers, lifeguards and other onlookers blown there by the wind.

He took a swig, already surrounded by a smiling group of topless lunch-break high-school girls. He handed it to the tall woman holding my hand, she took a hit, handed it to me and I passed it on. She nodded towards the crescent beach. Surfers were up on rollers. The thunderheads were nearly gone.

'I don't have a card on me,' I said, patting my ruined cutoffs, 'but my name is Cody Wallace, from Santa Flora, California.'

'My name's Peppi Harman,' she replied, squeezing my hand powerfully and not letting go. 'Thanks for saving my life.'

'Oh, I got a couple of free drinks out of it,' I said, casually consulting the watch on my other wrist, like in the payoff of a torture-test commercial. 'Could it be your lunch hour?'

'I seem to have nothing pencilled in,' she replied, so I disengaged my hand, reached round her shoulder (she was at least six-one, so it fitted snugly) and walked her away from the disaster area to the warm naugahyde spaces of my convertible.

The lilikoi flower was lying there and I passed it to her.

'*Passiflora edulis* Sims.'

She held it tenderly, then tucked the stem behind her ear.

A lot of cubic inches of engine snapped our vertebrae out of a storm-swept bay.

I snapped back the clasps of the roof and worked the power mechanism. 'Tell me about this life I've saved. How do *King Lear* and lifeguarding somehow interlock?'

'I'm on sabbatical,' she said in that recordable voice, bell-like and husky at the same time. More guardedly, she added: 'From Stanford drama department. I burned out.'

I settled down to fifty along the beachside highway under an emotionally purged sky. 'How does it go? *And for the book of knowledge fair, presented me with a universal blank . . . ?*'

The touch of her eyes was on me as we crossed the coastal plain with tall sugar cane all around waving Hi! at the blue.

'That's Milton,' she objected.

'Milton who?' I replied with an arched brow, and she gave me an 'old' look.

The Waianae range came into view round the headland like a fact into a conversation, jutting crisp and virginal into the squeaky-clean atmosphere. The Peppi Harman high-beam stayed on me, relaying mystic co-ordinates to command centre as I drove.

'We both need a clean up,' she stated after a minute or two. 'My place is not far. Let's go there.'

Seconds ticked by as her words spread warmth down my pleasure zones.

'Must be the rugged profile,' I said eventually.

'Let's say I have shares in Mister Big 'n' Tall.'

'Okay, but be kind.'

5

SHE directed me down a lane which forked off where the highway cleared the canefields near the shore. The lane ran along the rear of an old-established residential waterfront strip shaded by coconut groves.

Her garden gate was haloed by a cloud of cottonwood fluff. We went through it to a guest cabin constructed mostly out of driftwood. Wisteria cascaded round a pair of sunbleached French doors. There was a warm, secluded patio which faced across a lawn towards a shuttered-up colonial shingle home half-hidden in a clump of palms and breadfruit trees. Beyond it the sea flashed promising messages and surf hissed cleanly out at the reef.

I gave the cabin the professional once-over.

'Early Robinson Crusoe with some later Man Friday influence.'

'Let's get those dirty pants off,' she said in a motherly way, 'and wash those termites out of our hair.'

It was strange to find myself showering in the little stall off Peppi Harman's bedroom, when an hour earlier I had been casting around for a way to talk. When I came out, with my shorts back on, she was padding about barefoot-naked in the kitchenet cutting up melon and papaya flesh, green and pink. An uncapped bottle of Kirin was waiting: I met it. She turned and snaked her arm around my neck, the big kitchen knife in her hand travelling round my scalp and reappearing beside my ear.

What with grief and disease and silver threads among the gold, I'd been sublimating desire into the California wine industry for several years. Now a naked goddess smelling of fresh-cut tropical fruits was nuzzling me chastely as a reward.

'We must stop meeting like this,' I muttered coyly.

'Fate threw us together,' she said in a Katharine Hepburn voice, letting her nipples gently stroke my chest.

'Is this a whirlwind romance?' I asked, looking into a wide-open sunlit glacier behind her eyes. 'I think I know why Saxons didn't mind being gored to death.'

'Death is the veil which those who sleep call life.'

'*Plus ça change.*'

We watched each other's souls laugh and wave a spiritual hand of recognition. Time skipped a groove. She bumped my bulge away with her pelvis.

'Be a duckie and lay the table.'

We sat cross-legged on Balinese scatter rugs at a bamboo coffee table decorated with the lilikoi blossom, devouring ryebread triple-deckers spilling over with cream cheese, bean shoots and sliced red pepper, with tall passion-fruit drinks on the side.

'So where you from, Cody Wallace?' she said, when we were on to the fruit.

'Santa Flora.'

'Never heard of it.'

'Named after Santa Claus's ex-wife.'

'Is it one of those missions north of Big Sur?'

'The original.'

'So are you descended from Buffalo Bill or did your mother just go in for cowhands?'

'Several incarnations ago. Arizona. She married the mansion.'

It came back quickly, vulnerably, the blue glacier misting over, lids descending like storm clouds.

'You married?'

'I was. According to your Shelley quote she fell asleep and came to life. My version is, I nursed her through cancer and buried her on the beach in 1985.'

She digested it for a moment, face falling.

'How harrowing for you. I'm sorry.'

We looked into each other's real faces, the kidding gone.

'Don't be. You remind me of her.'

The crinkly smile she gave me wound up Reel One of the Wallace Story. Until that turning point it had been Since Laurie. Now, although I only half realized it, Anno Peppi had begun. She asked gently: 'What was she like?'

'Funny. Lonely. Generous. Tall – ' I stopped. The old lonesome ache for Laurie was never far away.

Peppi shone the blue ray all over me, reached across the table and pulled my hands over to cushion them against her breast.

'You got love in you, Cody Wallace!'

'Hey, cool it,' I joshed.

'What's the time?'

We both checked my wrist.

'AD One. Year One. Day One,' I said.

She got up and went to the door. It was a great sight, her and the door.

Over her shoulder she said: 'Come on, I'll show you something.' Seeing me hesitate, she added: 'Don't need my bathing suit, there's no one.'

She padded down the garden, her peach-like behind leading me past the owner's plantation-style residence, across more lawn, through a clump of eucalyptus and cottonwood, onto a deserted beach made of sand like white sugar. The reef was thirty yards out, enclosing an opalescent coral lagoon.

A scene hard to improve on, but Peppi wading naked into the water achieved it.

We swam across the lagoon with vivid fishes darting below. Peppi showed me a way to climb up onto the coral, face the ocean and dive into a sprawling wave, crawling strongly ahead to plunge neatly under the next as it broke from twenty-foot high. She disappeared for a moment, and came bobbing up the other side with her hair slicked down.

Familiar with the scope of her dips, I shook my head when she beckoned, and she headed out to sea alone, riding on controlled, mile-eating crawl strokes.

Joined In Holy

I went back and flopped on the blinding sand, trying to force coherence onto a massive decision which was making me tremble.

6

PEPPI could swing the days off, so I went to her shack at 6.45 am next day and we flew in a plane painted with huge flowers to the isle of Maui, where I took her in a Hertz Mercedes to the summit of Haleakala, ten thousand and twenty-three feet.

'Which plus the two of us is ten thousand and twenty-nine feet,' she said as we got out. It was noon in bright sun and we were wearing sweaters.

It took us an hour of gawping, just to start to comprehend the scale of the crater; the force that had blasted Maui up from the floor of the sea seven miles underfoot; the breadth of the sky with last night's half-moon fluffy white in the east and the sun a yard closer overhead; the way the summits of the other islands poked out from a blissful haze on the ocean, far off in an empyrean dream, a hundred leagues from anywhere.

'This is where I could sound my barbaric yawp over the roofs of the world,' I said, holding all of Peppi Harman and letting the Pacific sirocco blow my brains out through my ears.

She was gazing across my shoulder, murmuring. I put my ear close and picked up the words across the airstream. They were: 'Two red roses across the moon.'

We walked the crater, a mile-wide basin of moonscape, trying to grasp the idea of plate tectonics, earth's molten core and its explosive crust. She talked about Mount St Helens and the mothballed atom plants of Washington. I talked about Mont Ventoux and the sixty-five planned atom plants of France.

'There's two on Ventoux, which blasted in the 1700s,' I said.

'That's a few seconds ago,' she replied.

'Reactors are deadly for a quarter of a million years.'

'They're nuking Mururoa atoll.'

We shared hatred of France for a while.

The far rim of Haleakala's crater turned out to be the right place. Climbing up over it, we sat at the summit of the longest scree imaginable. It plunged near-vertical five miles into the sea. Or maybe it zoomed five miles out of it. Whichever way, you held on.

'I feel guilty, driving up here,' Peppi said after a long communion with the wind. 'It's too much to get for too little effort. How long would it take to climb?'

I said: 'Let's kidnap the head of the French nuclear testing program, lash him to a wagon wheel and roll it off here. How long would it take to go down?'

'How high would he bounce on the way?' Peppi mused.

I said: 'He'd enter the water at two hundred miles an hour.'

'The centrifugal force,' Peppi said, 'would drive the blood out through his pores.'

I said: 'When at last he resurfaced, he'd be suspended face down below the wheel and have his flesh slowly flayed by carnivorous fish.'

'Or he might float face upwards,' Peppi said, 'and have his eyes pecked away by seagulls.'

I said: 'I wonder if he'd understand.'

We sat hugging our knees for an hour, occasionally wiping the wind-tears off our cheeks. Suddenly Peppi put her arm round me.

'Let's do things, Cody.'

'We'll start an eco-army of two.'

I drove her to Kahului. It was a coming out of orbit, a wrenching away from the numen of the volcano. We sat drinking steam beer in a Wild West bar that had Japanese management, and I asked about her background.

'My mother works with Mother Teresa,' she said.

'She's a doctor?'

'Was, but got over it. Now she's a healer. Owns a palace near Calcutta where she runs an orphanage, but her main thing is healing small children who've been crippled by their parents to make them better beggars.'

'She's a faith healer.'

'We don't call it that. Too fundamentalist. We keep faith out of it.'

'Just keep the faith.'

'Healing is what it is. She baptizes a crippled child, a healthy child walks out of the river.'

'I'm surprised the whole of India isn't gathering on the shore.'

Her eyes saucered. 'Oh, but they do, every year. At Benares. Mother is always there.'

The sun was going down. I drove her to Lahaina. We sat on a deck over the water looking west. The table napkin was white linen, the service heavy silver; there was an orchid in the vase, a scattering of other guests, and a bottle of Montrachet in the bucket. We used it for a toast: 'To the Pooka Shell.'

I almost put it to her, but the warm inner surf broke, striking me dumb. Swordfish steaks were brought, and she told me about her father as we toyed with them.

'Daddy is an alchemist,' she said carefully. 'He is a student of Hermes Trismegistus, the Byzantine philosopher.'

'Magician?'

'If you like.'

'I like.' The whole room suddenly seemed on fire. 'Look at that sun give up the ghost,' I murmured.

She turned. Her profile was the only sight that could have torn my eyes away from the curling smoky crimson crisis happening over the isle of Lanai.

'If the doors of perception were cleansed,' she said, 'man would see everything as it is, infinite.'

She watched the sun die. I watched her watching. She turned, and I opened my mouth to say it. A puff of mist made her shimmer.

She laid a long forefinger gently against my parted lips. 'Never seek to tell thy love,' she whispered, 'love that never told can be, for the gentle wind does move silently, invisibly.'

Later we took the nearest twin room overlooking the water, threw open the balcony doors and windows, lay naked in bathrobes, one a bed. She had a repertoire of nonsense songs. I got the 'Quangle Wangle's Hat' and the 'Owl and the Pussycat' in full.

Morning came easily, and she was gone.

I found her later, coming out of the sea in a black string bikini.

'Even with you there, I hate the shore,' she told me, towelling down.

We drove to Hana, which is saying something, because as Peppi observed when we were an hour in: 'If they didn't want us to get there, why the hell did they build the highway?'

Ninety-nine hairpin bends later, each one hugging the foot of sheer cliffs, teetering over jagged rocks and a breaking sea, we arrived on the tiny shelf we had seen from miles in the sky the previous day. This was Hana, millionaires' hideaway, a place for hyper-rich hermits – who came in by chopper, as I realized too late.

The sole road took us along dry-stone walls built of round lava rocks, among papaya groves heavy with fruit. It petered out at the foot of the Hana valley, an Eden which had sprouted out of raw cooling crust on the flank of Haleakala.

Among blossoming poinciana and candlenut there were meadows bordering a stream, the grass an unreal shade of brilliant green. A thick waterfall filled a cleft in the mountain wall, and a vivid rainbow hovered over it. Peppi wandered around plucking at the grass and came to me with a posy of little mushrooms with caps like brown nipples. She was peeking across them at me with a joke in her eye.

The mushrooms' cosmic giggle caught up with us halfway through the coastroad ordeal, and it took us a couple of lifetimes to make it as far as the first stretch of road which went more than fifty yards without a U-bend. When the time came, I could barely hold the Merc on a straight stretch.

Peppi kept groaning, fighting to recover her gravitas and saying, 'I think I've peed my pants.'

We entered Kaenae paranoid. But a bar called Gunsmoke took our money in exchange for beer and left us to howl into the suds with no sweat.

Later we lay all laughed out in the waterfront room, watching patterns flowing on the ceiling.

After a long time, Peppi sat up and looked out across the sea. Then she checked above her.

'Uh, Cody, there really are patterns on the ceiling,' she said. 'It's a three-quarter moon. On the water. Reflecting.'

I sat up on my elbows and nodded sagely.

'Yep, the dream is the world. Will you stay with me for ever?' Out it came.

Leaning towards me, she gave a little shrug, loosening the bathrobe and swaying her breasts in their cave. We were virgins together, but her body was marked for me.

'I'm here, aren't I?' she said lightly, and lay down, pulling a sheet over her.

We let the sea hush lull us. And with the help of a little warm sake, slept.

In the morning, she was in my bed.

'No, Peppi,' I said, very gently, but the way I meant it. 'I want us to marry, have a honeymoon.'

She rolled away and regarded me, curious, amused, blushing. 'Is that how it is?'

'I imagine you've tried everything else.'

'There's no other way I can get my hands on you?'

I shook my head, and there was a delighted gonging, followed by a hum, as Peppi laughed. During the long pause that followed, the blue glacier rayed me from my hair to my chin, down round my shoulders and chest to my crotch and my legs, then worked back up until it locked with my eyes and started gently nodding.

'Okay.' She crossed to the other bed and pulled the sheet up. 'Will it take long?'

I reached for the phone.

'Married?' Hans Regner, my friend and landlord, echoed. 'Witnesses? Come and see me about it, I can't think straight right now. I've been burgled.'

7

HANS beamed and threw his arms wide. 'Will you look at this, Ilsa!' He was greeting us on his verandah dressed in full Rider Haggard rig, consisting of a tawny safari shirt tailored for him at Abercrombie & Fitch in about 1924, knee-length Empire-wallah shorts, khaki kneesocks folded down once, canvas hiking boots, and on his broad wrist a prewar Tissot watch which he treasured for its Roman digits which glowed cancerously green in the dark. His master-race head leaned back to appraise Peppi, with the expression of one pedigree individual recognizing another, the undimmed gray eagle-eyes immediately admiring. Regner felt twenty, acted forty, looked sixty and was actually eighty-two.

Sober-faced Ilsa, half his age, was hanging back, wearing the usual plain Prussian twinset and white deck shoes. To create a festive effect she appeared to have taken a brush to her soup-bowl economy haircut.

'Extreme old age forces us to live each day as we should, like our last,' Regner said, lightly taking Peppi's hand and bowing to kiss it, his weather-beaten face flushed with pleasure. On the way back to Mokuleia Beach we'd dropped in at our respective huts and changed: she looked even taller, almost willowy, in a Grecian-urn-style sleeveless gown, tied with a plaited sash. I'd pulled on my cream safari suit, Haida silverwork bracelet and sandals to strike a harmonious classical note.

My throat constricted, seeing the old man so taken. I was

27

strangely susceptible. Escorting Peppi after our conversation of that morning had given me an inner melting sensation all day. Warm desire-surf kept beating at my walls. Edges of me blurred in the spray.

Regner took charge of her. He'd lowered the fly blinds on his verandah and an array of candles burned unwaveringly over four places set round one of Ilsa's mango gazpacho soups. He steered Peppi to the place of honour beside the head of table, seating her in front of a baked snapper that lay in a nest of broken yams dressed with a glazed honey sauce. On one side was a ewer of sliced papaya dressed with chunks of lime, on the other a tray stacked with *poi* and its steamed leaves, *luau.* Regner toasted us in Kirin beer and announced that he and Ilsa would be proud to witness the ceremony.

'Cody Wallace has been a widower too long!' he said.

Over coffee, when we'd stripped the fish to a comb and moved across the verandah to battered davenports, Regner asked Ilsa to blow out the candles and announced he would be telling a ghost story in honour of our marriage. Peppi shifted closer to me. The Regners were strange enough.

'In 1928 we were botanizing in the Fijian islands,' the distinguished voice began, its owner little more than a shadow against the grille blind. 'Our explorations took us to a remote island far out in the archipelago where there were ancient temples, and people who preserved the old customs.

'One of the profoundest beliefs of these traditional Fijians was in *mbulu*, a heaven which they considered far better than earth – so much better that they had no doubts about going there. In fact it was considered a favour to dispatch somebody over to the other side.

'At a shrine we met a tall young man about twenty years old who looked a bit off colour, but not particularly starved. He was rolling up his mat, obviously going away, and we asked him where. To which he replied that he was going to be buried.

'We told him he was not dead yet. He replied that he would be after he'd been buried. So why was he going to be buried? He said it was days since he'd eaten anything and if he got any thinner the women were going to laugh and point and call him skeleton man.

'Who was his birth god, we asked. The shark. Could the shark not help? Oh, yes. If he went swimming the sharks would not eat him.

'Could they not give him an appetite? He shrugged. A white man would never understand. Being laughed at by women was total degradation.

'By this time, his family were waiting at the door. The father had a wooden spade, mother had on a new bark-cloth suit for the occasion, and the sister had a whale's tooth for him to hold by way of introduction to the great god Ragga-Ragga.

'Off he went, with the relatives following, laughing and joking on the way. When we got to the cemetery his father set about digging a grave. The sister covered her brother in lampblack to make him invisible in the Underworld. The mother helped him into a new bark-cloth suit and took what messages he had for absent friends. There were nose-rubbings all round. Then he asked for a last cup of water.'

Regner's silhouette took a sip of brandy. He went on:

'Father, tired out with digging the grave, started fretting and grumbling about what a nuisance the boy'd been all his life, and now what a nuisance he was making of his death. But the drink was fetched.

'After having the drink, the boy said he'd noticed vines overhead. He thought they looked good for strangling and he'd prefer to be strangled.'

Hans paused. There was only the hush of the distant surf.

'The father started shouting at his son to die like a man. He hopped around in a fury and eventually, as a kind of concession, jumped into the grave and spread a mat. The boy gave in and lay down in the hole with his hands clasped across his belly, holding the whale's tooth. The mat was wrapped round him and about a foot of earth was shovelled in.'

Hans paused again. Peppi's hand found mine.

'The father jumped in and stamped the earth down on the boy, shouting "*Sa Tiko, Sa Tiko, Sa Tiko*" – stay there, stay there!

'We stood and listened. A stifled moaning and choking could be heard. They shovelled in more earth, another foot of it, and the father stamped it down, shouting out "Goodbye", and we listened again. This time it was hard to be sure. Everybody had trooped down to the stream for a wash. But the boy's presence – he'd been standing there having his drink a few moments earlier – haunted the clearing.'

Hans's shape leaned forward.

'Impossible not to go back to that fresh grave. The noise of the relatives had faded away. I stood close. There was a silence . . . '

Surf clumped in the distance.

' . . . but I swear I could still hear him, moaning under the ground.'

Ilsa made a dismissive noise and switched on a table lamp. Regner was sitting there relishing his effect, mischief twinkling in his hooded old eyes.

'And in what way is this story appropriate for a wedding?' I asked.

'Heaven, my boy,' Regner came back suavely, rising from his chair. 'Think of faith. Think of heaven.' He turned to Peppi. 'Would you care to see some botanicals?'

'Hans, what about the break-in?'

He waved a hand. 'It was more like a search than a theft. God knows, Ilsa doesn't have many baubles, but the few things she keeps in a drawer by the bed were untouched. The guns weren't taken.' He shrugged, with a wink at Peppi. 'Could it be the work of a delirious botanist driven mad with jealousy over my achievement of forty years ago?'

When the study tour was over we thanked the Regners, promising to confirm the time of the ceremony, and I drove a mile down the coast to a spot where we could park open-topped at the edge of the beach. We looked out to sea, each of us sensing how much better we felt living on earth than lying suffocating under it in the name of a dream.

After a while we looked away from the sea. The moon laid a glittery trail across the ocean, up the hood, through the wind-shield to silver the side of Peppi's face, shining at me out of her eye.

'This is crazy, but it fits,' she murmured. 'It's time I started a new life. I've been drifting.'

With my heart singing, I reached out to touch a galaxy. 'To hell with four-star hotels, I have a million-star automobile.'

Joined In Holy

'How much longer?' she asked.
'Licence tomorrow. Ceremony Saturday.'
'Is kissing okay?'
I said it was.
It was.

8

THEY took her next day.

Maybe something deep inside me expected it, as if happiness attracts misfortune. Just a few generations ago Hawaii had been a kind of paradise, and it was permeated with a sense of loss. I sat on the beach that morning idly reading about it while nervously keeping watch on the lifeguard on the beach chair. Her outfit became imprinted on my memory. She was wearing a white tennis hat, green-chevroned white tracksuit top and pink track-suit pants.

I only got through a few pages of a photographic guide to the Polynesian Cultural Center. Heaven evidently had its down side. The way they told it, taboo, the Hawaiian religion, seemed to have been a flawed philosophy. Women dressed in grass skirts and nothing else had been servants of men from the Day God Created the World until the Morning Methodist Missionaries Arrived. Within days the whole setup had collapsed. The dusky swaying breasts were strapped into corsets, hula dancing gave way to hymn singing and the ladies sat down to dine with the gents. Nobody likes to be taboo. Especially not for twenty thousand years.

There was plenty for Peppi to do. She helped a fellow lifeguard to launch the rowboat while the surf was in a lull, so he could row out to tinker with the line of orange buoys that was supposed to keep swimmers from being run down by ski boats. She took a mother to find her lost toddler. She did some deck chair counting. She got relieved for a break and swam to the horizon and back. She did push-ups, pumped iron and played parallel bars. Once she went to the office for a long time about the arrangements for leaving at short notice and I was on my feet when at last she reappeared.

In her lunch break Peppi played volleyball with the beach staff, who'd heard about us marrying and going to live in California and had arranged a sendoff party for next day. I nursed a cold beer fetched from the corner store and watched the game. When she went up on chair duty I cleaned out the car ready to hand it back to the rental office, then lay on the sand again until at last my 3.30 rendezvous was near. I got up and made a ball of my book, coconut oil, Trident gum and towel and, waving cheerfully, walked over to my rentawreck. She blew me a kiss as I drove away.

Soon I was tooling inland through slashed sugar cane and pineapple plantations, over the central plain of Oahu, to the garrison town of Wahiawa, where a cordial municipal lady was waiting with a marriage licence.

After stopping off at a travel agent and at the local branch of the Pacific Interstate Mutual Savings & Loan, I was soon escaping the shimmering expanses of blacktop back into rolling fields, passing down through the picturesque shantytown of Waialua to Mokuleia Beach where I'd been renting the top of a garage from the Regners, an on/off habit for the best part of a decade since a chance meeting with Hans at the christening of a botany wing I'd designed at Berkeley.

Ilsa expected me to pay the rent on the button every week in five-dollar bills or smaller. This time it was a personal delivery: I was signing off. The wedding was to take place eight hours before my fixed-date return ticket expired, and I'd secured a seat for Peppi on the same flight.

Ilsa was waiting at the table on my verandah, and accepted the envelope I handed her, counting out the bills right there, with me watching in some amusement. Ilsa's upbringing in wartime Berlin still made every US greenback a tangible symbol of salvation.

'Ilsa, you should tuck them in your bra next to your heart.'

33

She finished the count and let the cool dark eyes come up. The usual dun-coloured blouse and skirt and sensible lace-up shoes did nothing for her. She was one of those even-featured women with good skin who in their mid-forties could have looked better than ever. But she was too serious, and my cute remark needed putting straight.

'I used to scour the Kurfürstendamm for discarded scraps of anything that could be sold,' she muttered, reciting from a treasured litany of pain. 'Many times I pulled the mittens off the frozen hands of a corpse to barter them. There would be children like me waiting and shivering while down some alley their mothers were being used like bitches by big Mongolian butchers in long gray coats. One after the other, they lined up to use them, paying a few pieces of stale Red Army bread, or a brass button stolen from a Reichswehr corpse. A woman might be accepting buttons torn from the coat of her own man, killed defending each square metre of the city.' She stared gravely down a bleak corridor of memory. 'Those mothers longed for death. Only the hunger of their children stopped them jumping into the Spree.'

I made a commiserating noise. 'You're on the other side of the world now, Ilsa.'

She mused almost tenderly: 'Every woman and girl was raped. It was systematical, you see. The victors wanted to breed a new race off the crushed Germans. Little half-Russians, half-Mongols, half-Georgians.'

'Not an urge I ever understood – until recently,' I said.

'Rape?' she remarked balefully. 'I hope not.'

'No. Something equally primitive. Little half-Codys.'

She frowned. 'But you and Laurie could have adopted.'

I said nothing back. Jagged pieces of grief inside me had worn themselves down into a fragile order I did not wish to disturb.

She watched me pursing my mouth. Hans married her for the eyes, I thought. They were so . . . *organized*. And something rare was happening. The organization was amused.

'Why Codeee! I do believe you're broodeee!'

'There must be an instinct,' I blustered, feeling my face

flushing, 'or we wouldn't be making an ant hill out of the planet. Didn't you ever want kids yourself?'

'With a man nearly forty years older?'

'The choice was yours.'

She pulled a wry face.

'My circumstances were unusual, a family was the last thing I had in mind. Hasn't Hans told you about us in your all-night whiskey sessions?'

'The gist of it. You corresponded for years. Met at a conference. He swept you out of the clutches of Uncle Joe.'

'The part you miss out is that he never knew what gender I was.'

'All in the cause of science?'

'Exactly. He presumed anybody with my expertise in botany had to be a man. In ten years of correspondence with this revered figure, I used only my initials and kept it strictly professional. So he couldn't analyze my handwriting, I went to a lot of trouble to get access to typewriters. Only officials were allowed them, but I was determined never to write longhand.'

'Why?'

'His male prejudice would have instantly discounted my work. Hans was the authority on my subject, it was a matter of academic survival. Also he was married – most of that time.' She stared at her hands, tangling and untangling the fingers. 'The botanical conference of 1967 was to be held in East Berlin, first contact since the Wall had gone up. I couldn't miss it. The authorities were watching me. Oh,' she snorted, 'a correspondence between a junior researcher – a woman to boot – and an American expert was considered quite impertinent.'

'They interfered?'

'After the first year or so none of his letters and parcels arrived unopened. Some of mine never got to him. Finally,' she shook her head, 'finally they tried to prevent me attending the conference. Such stratagems! Like wicked schoolboys!' She gazed away, as if the threat was somewhere out there still.

'Surely botany's not a high-security science?' I said. 'Why the pressure?'

She arched an eyebrow. 'Have you any idea how much

modern pharmaceuticals owe to botany? And anyway,' she added, getting up and poking my rent money into her blouse pocket, 'Hawaii is crammed with military electronics, strategically positioned at the crossroads of the Pacific. Don't you think the idea of me escaping and settling here gave a Prussian Stalinist heartburn?'

'It's good to know things've loosened up now,' I said hopefully, but her lip curled.

'Nothing changes,' she muttered coldly.

'The Wall's down,' I objected.

'And the gulags?' she said.

The clank of Ilsa's distant cell doors jarred with my upbeat mood. I steered her back to matrimony. 'So Hans met you in person, took one look and popped the question.'

She shrugged some of the weight off herself. 'Not exactly. He had his male version of me lined up to become coauthor for the final volumes of *Pacifica Floriensis*. The female me came as a bit of a letdown.'

I gave her a look. 'Come off it.'

'But he'd just been widowed. That helped a lot. It swung him.'

'Swung me,' I said.

She went to the stairs. 'Come play chess with Hans tonight. He dreads you going back. He's actually in Pearl Harbour right now looking for the *Chung Mee* – he wants to recommission her and sail off on another expedition.'

I declined the invitation: jawboning with Doctor Hans Regner all night had to be prepared for, physically and mentally. Urging her to remember to keep Saturday open, I vaulted into the car and accelerated along the coastal highway, thrusting old European hatreds behind me, gravitating towards the lifeguard chair on Waimea Bay like a steer to a salt lick.

Shame, when I turned into the car park, that a couple of lifeguards ran out from the office waving, and that when I was half out of the car the taller one, burnt to chocolate, with a white rubber skullcap over his crew cut, called out: 'That buncha hillbillies came down the Scout Camp trail and hauled Peppi off in their truck. She tell you she had a date with them? Reckon we should call the sheriff?"

And shame that, with electric shocks jangling my body, I already knew what they were shouting over my roaring engine – 'Short-box 50s Ford! Longhairs with a rack a guns!' – and a black claw gripped my heart, making my limbs move robotically, spinning my power steering back in the direction of Mokuleia Beach with rubber screeching in my soul.

I gripped the wheel and held steady, as if any lurching or veering from my purpose might somewhere tip Peppi over. Car horns brayed by. A blue panel truck caught trying to cross bounced and blundered off the highway into a pineapple field.

Peppi dived naked into the surf beyond the windshield. Under the surf lurked sharks. I stamped on the gas like a hard-rock drummer working his bass drum. Mokuleia Beach arrived along my own private wire.

Hans Regner stood frozen halfway up his path where he'd pirouetted on hearing my locked wheels ploughing gravel. He had rocket-site shades on: I talked into my own reflection. Already there were two of me. I was cloning into a posse.

'Peppi got snatched.'

The two of me bucked.

'Snatched? Who by?'

'Dope farmers. Raper geeks. She's in trouble. Going after them. Need a weapon, any kind.'

'Wouldn't you do better to contact the sheriff and get his men onto it? I'm sure there's some reasonable expla – '

'Fer Chrissake, Hans, give us a break from that shit!'

He still didn't move.

'Oh, fuck it.' I pushed past him.

Ilsa was out on the verandah.

'Emergency,' I panted, topping the stairs and dodging by her, hauling the storm door open and heading down the hallway.

I halted at the centre of the worn Indian carpet in the green glade of Hans's study. One wall was racked with the tools of his trade: heavy plant presses, press paper, sample sacks, backpacks, climbing boots, compasses, cameras, rolled charts, maps and the like. Ranged round the other walls were books at all angles, with sheaves of papers stuffed on top of them in organized confusion.

Fifty years' work in this room had earned him three plants with *Regnerius* in their names at the New York Botanical Garden. On a side table stood a crowd of framed pictures in which pith-helmeted Regner towered over corpulent ratus in skirts. Over the wide Morocco desk strewn with books and papers there was a painting of his hundred-foot junk-style schooner, the *Chung Mee*, and a couple of framed academic certificates with red wax seals. Beside them was the glass-fronted gun cabinet.

I picked up a jade Buddha from the picture table and threw it at the glass. The impact brought relief, as if the jangling, cascading shards represented a cockeyed world falling into place.

There were four drawers under the barred-up rifles and shotguns. I pulled the top left one open and brought out a bundle of green baize cloth. Wrapped in it was a heavy revolver of classic design, an old ·38 Webley of British Empire officer-issue vintage. Hefting it in my right hand, I used my left to pull out the top right drawer, then the lower left, then the lower right. No ammunition. I started on the drawers of Hans's Morocco-inlaid desk. In the third one I tried there were boxes of cartridges. At last I found a box marked ·38. I snatched it up and turned to the door.

Hans filled it, the eyes seething black holes, the big, ancient frame irresolute.

'What you got, Cody? Sunstroke? Don't scoff, it happens. And put that thing down, those drug dealers're hard cases. Let Sheriff Quilley take care of it.' Age rattled in his broad old chest.

'Hans, I don't want to say this, but you're an old man, and I'll break you.'

He bared his teeth in a rictus of distress, and I tipped bullets onto the desk, hurriedly fingering them into the Webley's cylinder.

When I clicked the gun shut Ilsa was there behind him. 'Phone the sheriff,' he wheezed, bracing himself against the doorjamb. She disappeared.

I scooped other bullets into my pocket and made for the door. Hans gave way, fighting for breath.

There was no police intercept the whole way back, but as I cornered out of Waimea Bay, narrowly avoiding collision with an oncoming coachload of early Japanese tourists, I still overshot the turn-off, hung a squealing U-turn and went back in the opposite direction at 60 mph. That way I was sure there was no tail on me when I took the Scout Camp trail.

9

REFLECTED in my driving mirror the sun was making a huge statement about birth, death and the galaxy as it lingered over the Waianae mountains, but I was blind to beauty. The death of light in tints of orange, sepia and purple seemed like part of a conspiracy.

Happiness is a restricted substance. The stoics were right: accept the law of nature and you'll be rewarded. I accepted it. My beauteous condition had been a magnet for ugliness. I fishtailed through bends as if I was being paid to chase the day over the edge of the world.

The ocean made a vast, blank gesture to infinity on my left. I kept my eyes fixed on the tarry ribbon ahead which led into dusky, unwelcoming hills.

The evening air coursing into my window, which on another night might have made me sigh with its scents and waftings, seemed used up and oppressive. I braked into the bends, sending Regner's pistol skidding into the passenger footwell so that I had to bend down and scoop it up. Twice the nearside wheels beneath me bucked over the edge of near-vertical screes. Twice I cheated them back again.

With the car roof closed for better aerodynamics it took me twenty minutes to reach the white observatory dome which surveyed the ocean's magic cloak of indigo, damask and vermilion, flanked by the white cigar tubes five storeys high, a dual Apollo mission emerging from the earth. The car reined back

like a bronco in front of the five-bar gate and its headlights made
the Scout Camp sign scream. I jumped out into rubber fumes
and inspected the padlock.

It was a stout brass unit stamped with the name of a foundry
in Cleveland, Ohio. The retaining rings were bolted right
through the metal gate and concrete post. A Rambo might have
rammed the gate, written off a car and broken his ribs. Vaulting
the bars and sprinting up the trail seemed like a possibility for a
second or two, except I had no notion of where I was headed or
how far. Me after ten miles would not be dangerous. Me after
one mile. I turned back to the car.

The blast hissed and jetted to and fro across the valley, up
and down, in and out, scouring clusters of birds up in silhouette
against the emerging stars above the saddleback. When I looked
down through the vapour drifting from the Webley's barrel, the
lock was dangling open.

I accelerated through the couple of miles of rough paddocks,
watched in the gloom by a few downhearted brindled ponies.
Soon higher hills reared on either side, all uninhabited. The
trail crossed a plateau and entered another, steeper valley. Miles
on in – had I really walked this far? – there was a T-junction
with a double finger post blazing in the light. I hauled up.
Leftwards it said Riding Stables. Rightwards it said Scout Camp.

When the dust cleared I could see through the gloom along
the Riding Stable route, up a long scrubland valley. Two sil-
houettes like stick insects shifted at the shoulder of a rocky
outcrop half a mile away. They were dwarfs, or little kids,
mounted on tiny track motorbikes. As I screwed up my eyes they
moved out of sight. A few seconds later angry little wasp-like
burps reached me and there was a plume of dust at the head of
the valley. I flung the car through the left turn, bouncing the
nearside wing off the signpost as I wrestled to correct.

The track took me surging westward over a saddleback which
commanded a vista of the Waianae range, now a black serrated
cutout against the fading aura of the sun. I plunged into a
shallow valley beyond, following a route into the foothills which
buttressed the high timber. I had to peer into the reaches of
my headlight span to try to second-guess a sudden bend or
unexpected precipice. Reaction time would be about one second.

It took three minutes to belly out the hollow and start climbing again. On this stretch it didn't matter if I fishtailed, the track was flanked by tufty banks which I could barge into. The wheels lodged in the storm ditches, but reckless oversteering wrenched me out. I went great guns, leaning forward, manically clutching the wheel, my pupils maxidilated.

With the auto stick shift rammed into second and the full force of my leg and heel pounding on the gas, I piled the Cutlass up to ninety as it took the gradient. Drainage culverts and fenced banks were a blur on each side as I approached the blind brow, so I stopped scanning the land for signs of habitation and concentrated on not flipping over and getting decapitated. But there was another problem.

It surfaced into view abruptly, like an apple bobbing out of water.

The baldy-headed contour of the roof bounced and swayed in jolly fashion. Old-fashioned radiator chrome danced a sexy boogaloo over the potholes. Dust furled up round the funky outline, with weird backlighting coming from the expiring day. During the long moment it took me to register what it was, the 50s short-box pickup seemed to be strung out in time, suspended, tapping out a rhythm on the earth with its tires. It was ninety yards away and there was no one at the wheel.

You could see the cab was empty, the purple sunset made an empty bean shape of the rear window through the windshield. The loop of the steering wheel stood out against the oval light each time the front wheels bucked against a rock. A ton and a half of high-quality vintage iron and steel, it had to be doing fifty miles an hour. Add my speed, get an impact velocity of a hundred and thirty. I was about to be processed into dog chow.

If I swung left or right the culverts would flip me. Braking would make me plane. My heart gulped for oxygen like a beached cod and my mind slipped mercifully away in a kind of faint.

A hand that belonged to me worked the nearest latch above the sunshield and reached to unfasten the one on the passenger side but we bounced and my body got thrown off balance. The other hand that belonged to me let go of the steering wheel. Now both vehicles were driverless.

The heels of both hands prized the other latch up and smashed against the brace, forcing the roof open to be ripped back by the airstream.

The night was an inspiration. I had broken through a brain as well as a roof. The body that was me waded a couple of steps across the seat, flailing its arms about in crazed semaphore, got one huaracho onto the door rim and took a leap into the unknown.

PART TWO

LET NO MAN PUT ASUNDER

10

THERE was a dull red planet, which if I let it go turned into bunched up pain and started unfurling. I tried to keep it as the deep heart of Peppi's body, holding it against me, so we could plunge around together in warm velvety depths, a spreading centre of unspoken knowledge, eternally private, unifying. But the red planet kept floating out, pulling me out of inner space back into pain. Each time I bore down on it, renewing my embrace of Peppi's heart, it pulled more strongly, tearing me away from cool black freedom into a throbbing haze which slowly focused into a voice, an unfriendly voice, the voice of the world, using my name.

'I think you c'n hear me, Wallace. There're some questions you gotta answer. Snap out of it.'

I thought it was me protesting in a gentle, womanly voice: 'Lieutenant, Dr Dewburg only authorized questioning provided that the patient was already conscious.'

My accuser came back: 'He opened his eyes. He said something. Wallace? . . . Wallace!'

Across a smear of pain I found myself looking at a face like the backside of an inhospitable planet, an acne-pitted desert with lumpy hills for chin, cheeks and brows, two missile silos for a nose and slanted oily lakes for eyes. The hair gleamed dully black like garbage bags.

There was not much movement at the thin line of mouth when the talking started again.

'Okay, Wallace, talk and things might go a titch easier. If you won't square with Honolulu Police Department you'll be dealing with the Feds and they won't take any wooden nickels. Okay – who you working for?'

The nurse was hovering behind him, clearly wanting him out of the way so that she could get at me with syringes, capsules, enemas. I preferred to let the darkness come back, only the red blur zoomed in again, and that was worse. I changed channel and let Oilyeyes and his flat Hawaiian-Chinese accent back into my life.

'Just tell me whose side you're on, Wallace. We can take it from there. You KGB? China? Commie Filipino? Sad Nadista?'

I pondered the last one and heard echoes of moonlight laughter.

'Where am I?'

My groaned query sent a pleasant beam of surprise into the nub of pain. Communication!

'University Hospital,' Oilyeyes imparted reluctantly, adding as a warning: 'In custody. Now out with it, Wallace. Who you working for?'

'He's confused, it's the concussion,' the nurse fussed. Oilyeyes held her back with an arm held out, showing the lousy cut of his gray suit.

A name swam up from the remains of comfort which lingered somewhere far inside me. I compared it with my anxiety. It matched.

'Peppi Harman.'

The pockmarked disc showed nothing.

'Peppi Harman,' I moaned again, wondering if I was actually speaking. 'What happened to Peppi?'

The name worked like a spell, slipping me back into the velvety comfort of clasping her by the matrix, caressing the world and feeling little eddies of pleasure wafting up and down my wand.

Ilsa Regner wakened me and I was there. I even hoped she'd brought food. After she'd kissed me anxiously I said: 'Where's the eats?' and she smiled with tears.

'Oh, thank Gott, Cody, you're better.'

'Hold it, I don't feel so hot.'

'Don't touch! Yes, your head's bandaged. And you've got contusions. They told me you were lucky.' The smile faded, to suit the way her hair was dressed in severe square bangs. A plain-faced, plain-dressed, plain-spoken Prussian peasant with penetrating eyes. To be studied by this woman was like getting a brain scan.

'Why did you do it?' she asked gravely.

'Where's Peppi? What happened to Peppi?'

'There's no Peppi.'

'What happened to her?'

'Nothing. She's gone. Forget her. Oh, Cody, why did you?'

My ribs screamed when I tried to jerk forward.

'Ilsa, why did I what?'

Her normally impassive face worked tragically.

'Don't make it worse, Cody. Tell them you lost control, tell them you were blackmailed . . . ' She broke off, startled at her own words. 'Were you? Are you in terrible trouble? We know so little about you, really. If you are, you can only make it worse this way. You must tell them everything.' Her eyes were darting, uncertain, she murmured after a moment: 'Haff you no memory of it?'

'A bunch of hoods snatched Peppi and took off with her into the hills. I got a gun from your place and followed them. As I was barrelling up the stables trail they sent their truck at me with the gas pedal and steering wheel lashed down. All I could do was bail out. I guess my car got totalled. I've been lucky. Nothing seems to be broken.' A pang came. 'Maybe a rib. My head aches. I'm hungry as hell. Where's Hans? Where's Peppi?'

With worried gray eyes fixed on me, Ilsa stretched out and pressed something near the head of the bed.

'So you never rammed the gates of the communications base?' The tone suggested I might not know what I was saying.

'What communications base?'

She patiently took a breath.

'Up towards Kaunala Ridge. There's a dome – '

' – a big white dome on top of a pod,' I chimed in. 'And a white cylinder beside it. A bunch of aerials, some breezeblock buildings. Gray gravel inside a wired compound. Heckuva view, way the hell and gone over the horizon. Yeah, I know it.'

The eyes were steadying out.

'You do remember.'

'Yeah, I thought it might be a telescope, but I never rammed the place. I shot the padlock off the gate behind it.'

'It's a top-security Federal installation, Cody. You smashed down the gates, crossed the compound and collided with a pair of iron doors leading to a prohibited area.'

My hands flexed, tugging at the drip feeds attached to the wrists. I could feel them gripping the windshield frame, see the white hood of my car, the crazy jerky motion of the robot truck in the corner of my eye, the green race of the culvert, and my heart bumped as I launched over the door again.

'No.'

'No?'

'No, I jumped out of my car. Everything went black. I just woke up now, although I do remember.'

'What d'you remember?'

'Don't look at me that way. I remember some guy with a hamburger patty for a face trying to do a ham-fisted fifth degree on me.'

'That'd be Lieutenant Lau.'

'Lieutenant?'

She nodded. 'Honolulu County Police Department.'

'Wow, you mean he was for real?'

'You've been unconscious. We – ' She bit her lip.

I waited.

'Yeah? We what?'

'We thought you might be lapsing into a coma.'

'I think the opposite's happening. I'm starting to wonder what's going on. I'm starting to wonder how you got involved in this, Ilsa. Where's Hans? And how did you get to know I was here considering that I didn't?'

'You put the studio address on the car-rental contract, Cody.'

'The car that was found wrapped round the doorpost of a Federal communications base.'

The eyes were steely.

'Yes.'

Maybe it was consciousness fully returning: suddenly the setup got to me, the bland sterility of a hospital, the insolence of the Hawaiian policeman, the disloyalty of my friend's wife. I was injured, and there was no information about Peppi Harman.

'Shit, Ilsa. I think I'm being fitted up. I don't know why and I'm not sure who by, but I do know I want to get out of this place – right now.'

She nodded enthusiastically, and shifted her chair closer to my bed.

'But that's just what Lieutenant Lau wants you to do, Cody. He told me he's prepared to let you go and drop all charges.'

'All charges. What charges?'

'Very serious charges, Cody.'

'How serious. What *is* this?'

'Well, they start with reckless driving and go right up to Federal charges of trespass, wilful damage and espionage.'

Blood blazed in my vision.

'Espio – '

' – Listen! They'll drop all charges if you leave here.'

Light started to dawn.

'Leave the state of Hawaii . . . '

She nodded, and I could read the story only too clearly in her steady, experienced gaze. She was a refugee who owed everything to Hans Regner, himself an immigrant who'd been impounded or exiled in two world wars. His victory over old age he owed to her, it was her doing. Her prime loyalty was to him, survival instinct made her act to shield him. It could mean life or death to the man in her life, a great man who had led her to paradise. I was his friend, but now I meant trouble, trouble the old man couldn't afford.

'You've come to see me off. I get it, when I said leave, I meant leave the hospital. You mean leave Hawaii.'

'We have often criticized the Government, Cody, fighting for the environment of the islands, which don't forget are America's Pacific base. We've been up against powerful people in the armed forces, the security services. They would jump at any chance of mixing us up in something like this.'

My dander rose again.

'Something like what?' I froze as synapses dovetailed together in my recovering brain. Ilsa watched as if she could see the connections being made in my face. 'You mean . . . '

'It could be a top-level setup,' she muttered, glancing over her shoulder at the glass-windowed door of my private room where a badged shoulder appeared for a moment, then moved out of view.

'To get at you guys,' I murmured back.

There were footfalls, the door window darkened, and hamburger head re-entered my life, looking more humdrum this time, more like a working stiff saddled with a dull task on what looked through the louvred blinds like a clear, sunny Pacific day. He was wearing another lousy suit, beige this time. It's hard to look elegant when you're about five-six and tubby. Ilsa rose to her feet respectfully.

'It's Interflora,' I growled.

He ignored me. The pair of them exchanged a wary glance and she said with amazing meekness: 'Mr Wallace agrees to leave the islands on the next flight.'

Lau laid oily almond-eyes on me and said: 'Who needs friends like that?'

Ilsa nodded – and her scenario fell into place for me. She figured Lau for a friend. A good cop, clearing up an oddball case the pragmatic way; refusing to collaborate with some harebrained frame-up devised by egghead superiors he despised. Helping to steer a distressed pair of German flowerpressers out of trouble.

'There's the little problem of my ticket,' I observed, winning their grudging attention.

'What about it, Wallace?'

'I hold a fourteen-day fixed tourist return. If you're going to kick me out of this state early on account of a bunch of cockeyed charges I'm damned if I'm going to cough up the price of a one-way ticket at maximum rate.'

Neither of them flinched, and I noticed that Lau had been followed into the room by a flunkey carrying my crush bag, which looked suspiciously as though it was full of things belonging to me.

'We know about your ticket,' Lau said curtly. 'Maybe you did, too, because you woke up just in time. You can still use it until midnight tonight. Now let's see you hang a leg out a that bed, brother, or I might just be changing my mind.'

Ilsa approached and braced me by the arm.

'Get nurses,' she snapped over her shoulder. Lau flicked his fingers at the flunkey, who dropped my bag and left.

'Hey, hey, hey, hey . . . he-e-ey,' I protested, smacking an invisible wall with splayed hands. 'Hold your horses. My fiancée is coming with me, and anyhow, my ticket doesn't come due till Saturday night. This is Wednesday. You're going to have to buy me and Peppi a ticket if you want . . . ' I trailed off, distracted by their blank expressions. 'What day is it, Ilsa?'

Something like fear tautened her face.

'It's Saturday, Cody.'

'You don't run your car at a pair of iron gates then take a catnap till happy hour, Wallace,' Lau sneered.

I felt dislocated, all right, but not the way they thought.

The latest traces of that wealth inside me pulsed up one more beam of hope that momentarily blew away my aches and pains.

I turned my splayed hands round and told them its name.

'Peppi. Where the hell is Peppi?'

The nurses came in and took over. Lau said I didn't need to eat because I had to get shaved and dressed. Everything hurt. They guided me through it like a lost child.

They let me have one call, but not until I was inside the departure lounge at Honolulu International, groggy on my feet on account of having been laid out for four days. I made the call to Sal.

'You're home.'

'Cody, nice to hear you. Yeah, well, I'm lookin' fer a job on account a the big bad wolf.'

'Sal, what's the story on Peppi?'

'She didn't show up for work all week. She's a flip case, man. You hear her recitin' po-try while the barroom was blowin' down? Shit!'

My mouth was open. I worked my throat. Nothing came.

'You uptight, Cody? Maybe she's staying with that friend, Della, along the coast a ways, Waialua. Down there.'

'Sal, I'm leaving for California. Something came up – '

'Yeah, I haven't seen you aroun'. I was wond'rin' . . . '

'Well, I'm at the airport right now and Peppi was supposed to be coming with me.'

'To California?'

'Yeah.'

'No shit!'

'Sal, are you high?'

'Hey, cool it, Cody. They bulldozing the Pooka, I haven't been down the beach. I reckoned Peppi'd taken off somewhere. Maybe with you.'

'We did see each other. A lot. We were going to – '

'You there, Cody?'

'Could you check around for me? Find out where the hell she is?'

I gave him my number in Santa Flora. He said he'd let me know what he found out. I laid my brow on the telephone rest. Lau had to take the receiver away.

Confusion, grief and the need to eat made me drivable, like a sheep. Lau and his spook drove me on board an empty 757, ahead even of the pregnancies and basket cases.

11

DURING the flight I consumed half a dishrag steak, two polystyrene lettuce leaves, three ounces of synthetic cream and a felt cracker. And five plastic cups of let's-pretend coffee. I felt too beat-up and ill after to think.

By the time we landed at San Francisco International I figured that if the whole scam had been a setup to snare a couple of has-been herbalists it was a honkout.

If, on the other hand, they genuinely suspected me of espionage they had a weird idea of protecting the Union.

What made me mad was, if the police believed the KGB was capable of blowing a mole by raiding a communications base as incompetently as I was supposed to have, those police must be outstandingly stupid. Even a police department couldn't be that dumb. Which made me scared as well as mad. And anyway, wasn't the Cold War supposed to be over?

Standing at the door of my Subaru 4 × 4 listening to a blistering roar from the runway through the barbed wire, I imagined turning back, getting a ticket to Honolulu and retaining an attorney, a private dick and a bodyguard to get my fiancée out of there.

I wish I had.

Instead I paid the ransom they took to release the jeep, and drove across the Montaras to Half-moon Bay, turning south along the coast for the thirty-minute run to Santa Flora, feeling

55

all the way like a traitor. But animal instinct drove me towards my kennel.

As a settlement Santa Flora doesn't change through the seasons, the hills always barge into the sea scrawny and barren, the occasional trees look lonesome and moody and don't-bug-me. The whore of an ocean keeps changing her dress to try to get a reaction.

On the main drag, which is squat and tacky, you reach for your shades to fight off the glare of Mercs, Caddies, Rollers and Porsches angle-parked outside the boutiques, most of them cloned versions of places on Cañon Boulevard. There was no sign of the poor bastards who'd once laid round the boardwalks, each of them the owner of a Nobel-prize-potential life story which in exchange for a fifth of hooch they'd spin out in gritty tones against the sound of Pacific rollers clumping onto the rocks.

My way lay through the center, another half-mile along the coast, passing beside sleek, low-key Mission villas until a hollow opened out in the hills to the left, suddenly green and rolling, with interesting clumps of shrubs here and knobs of turf there, to help the eighteen putting greens play harder to get. It was Laurie's brain wave and my design: Valle Verdosa, and I noted that the guys that owned it were running pretty loose with their sprinkler system in the middle of the afternoon, but that was their problem. Way down in the corner of it, perched on forty acres overlooking the bay, was the place I'd put up on the profits. It'd all been her idea, I took no credit, only revenue. For once, the remote worked on my garage door.

The Jaguar stood unstolen in the half-light, 1958, 3.4, British racing green. I patted the hood to say hi, and worked the house locks to open the connecting door to the den.

There were voices in the answerphone. Delbert Mann, West Coast editor for Doubleday, wanted me to call: any other time I would have got a warm literary glow, but I fast-forwarded past him. Abe Levene, manager of the condo, was inviting me over for drinks; he'd forgotten I was away. Fast forward. Clara Butt, neighbour, painter, drinking buddy and permanently miffed would-be lover, had left a laconic welcome home. It left me cold.

Sal's voice ran me colder.

'Cody, I've got this card to Peppi signed Mom. It was lying round her place. No sign of her there. The address is, got a pen? 3296 Diadem in Redwood City. I'll look up her friend Della tonight.' He signed off with: 'Later,' and the line went to dial tone. I reset the unit, stuffed the noted address in my pants pocket, pulled the phone off the charger and called directory. There was no Harman in Redwood City. The door buzzed.

When I opened it Abe looked me up and down like they'd delivered the wrong item.

'Your transplant job didn't work,' I said defensively.

'Baldness is sexy, I didn't get one. What happened? A Waikiki wipeout? A yarn to spin some drinks with on a rainy night?'

'It's nothing. A coconut hit me.'

Abe ran the condo because he'd accidentally made a million selling computer-patterned socks and liked the view. He speculated on world markets from five screens in his kitchen. When he appraised you, you felt like a downturning profit graph. I turned to the wall mirror.

'See what I mean?'

'Yeah, I saw in the john on the plane.'

I pulled the bandage off my scalp, threw my jacket away and went in for a wash. He followed me.

'I thought this was a picture book about old houses,' he said. 'And you were going to have a nice time sifting through photographs in the archives. Instead you look like gang murder.'

I kept washing dried blood off my temple.

'This lifeguard and I met in a hurricane. Later we went to Hana valley. We got high. It went weird. Someone talked about being buried alive.' The towel was soft and incredible. 'I got paranoid. She disappeared. I wrote off the car. The cops threw me out.' I checked Abe in the mirror. The story gagged him for two to three seconds.

'So what's with the ladyfriend? How come she's hot?'

I started clearing out my pockets on the vanity. There was a crumpled document. I unfolded it.

'What's that.'

'Marriage licence.'

'Uh-huh.' He took this in, nodding cautiously. 'So where she gone?'

'I don't know, Abe. What shall I do?'

He ran a big hand over his tanned scalp.

'Cops no good?'

'They shipped me out. Framed me. Covering something up.'

'Could be she's somebody important's tootsie, you should walk the other way, let her go.'

'No.'

'Not like that, this one . . . '

'I got to find her.'

Abe frowned. 'This is bad.' He liked a neat world of numbers strung like pearls on bottom lines. 'I guess you better check it out. You know her parents?'

There was a clean chino suit in the closet. Leaning most directions hurt, so it needed care to put it on. He followed me to the garage. Across the Jaguar I said: 'I have an address for someone who may be her mother. Then I'm going back to Hawaii. If I don't come back, please take the cat.'

He dwindled into the shade, reaching after me with one arm as I reversed away . . .

Redwood City is a joke name for twenty square miles of tract housing, but you do see traces of the dream in a few of the better quarter-sections. Along with the occasional traces of earthquake. Diadem Avenue crossed a humpback towards Cahill Ridge, clear of the hydrocarbon haze and commanding a view of the bay from among, yes, a scattering of scrawny redwood trees. It was executive territory which aspired to status, but a whiff of overstretched mortgages tainted the air.

3296 perched on a slope, a Prairie-style affair slabbed with floor-to-ceiling tinted plate glass, hugged by a three-bay carport and screened both sides by mature cypress hedges. There was an intercom plate by the gate below, with a plastic window displaying a printed card marked *Hedwig Rupert Maronek* in italic lettering. When I pressed the button, a slack female voice answered, and made the latch hum before I had got my name out. A shabby Toyota hatchback stood alone in the carport at the top of a steep drive.

It was my first electric sliding front door. The smoky tinting showed a ghostly figure, then the apparatus shifted leftwards into a slot in the wall, revealing a round-shouldered woman in her mid-forties, wearing shabby slacks and a corded tawny sweater with a V-neck you could drive down. She had Peppi's stature, but it slumped and sagged. Instead of being Viking, the face was jowly Danish, with boredom in the gray eyes and dereliction in the tumbling mouse-coloured hair. Even her pink-framed glasses, upside-down style, hung askew on her nose. If she was Peppi's mother, it only proved how hard nature keeps trying.

'Mrs Maronek?'

She sniffed. 'Mmmm.'

'Are you Peppi Harman's mother?'

She looked me up and down.

'Uh-huh.'

Something she did made the door close almost soundlessly behind me. I followed her hunched shoulders into a split-level living area, mostly glassed, with the view muted to sepia sky on one side and chocolate-coloured lawn and hedge the other. Two soap actors were mouthing limp nothings on a maxiscreen built into an oak-veneer wall unit. The other wall dominated the space: it was hung with a gallery of paintings brushed in lurid tints onto black velours. They were pictures of heartbroken children in a variety of outfits ranging from Hiawatha to Harlequin with many other shades of cliché on the way. Each had huge identical eyes glistening with outsize teardrops.

'Gee,' I said in genuine astonishment. It was a long way from here to Benares. Evidently Peppi's brain had built the bridge.

Her mother was lighting a Long taken from a ripped-open packet of two hundred. Empty and half-empty packs were strewn about the built-in davenports and over the fawn shag carpet. I guessed no one would hang such pictures in such numbers unless they had painted them, or whatever you did.

'You dating Penelope?' Mrs Maronek asked, her voice thickened with a hundred noxious vapours but devoid of concern.

'Yes.'

'She dump you? Siddown.'

I perched on the nearest corduroy pad.

'Peppi and I made friends while I was visiting Hawaii. I had some work to do over there and stayed on for a while. We met at Waimea Bay.'

'She visiting?'

The caring-mother–devoted-daughter tradition started crumbling. The room picked up the futility of the bland TV dialogue being muttered in the corner. A man was going to have a test-tube abortion but had to keep it a secret from his boyfriend. Something like that.

'Peppi's working over there.'

'Oh yeah?'

'She's a lifeguard.'

'Uh-huh.'

'Are you and she close? You wrote her, that's how I got your address.'

'Christmas card. Must've been forwarded. I sent them to Porter College. In Palo Alto.'

So much for Stanford.

She took a card off a stack on the coffee table and handed it to me between tar-stained fingers. A tearful Eskimo maiden pleaded for pity off the cover. The message stated: Have a Heart at Yuletide.

'A printer in Millbrae does them up, sells thousands to a chain in LA.' Hard to sound bored and proud at the same time, but she managed it. 'How come you reading Penelope's mail?' she demanded.

'Peppi's in trouble.'

'What kinda trouble?'

She rapped it back fast. Trouble was her ground.

'She got snatched off the beach by a bunch of heavies.'

'Shit, they'd prob'ly be friends o' hers. Actors, most likely. Sounds like the kind she was hanging out with up at San Francisco State.'

She said it with a kind of relish, bohemian solidarity and all that, but something more complicated jarred. Envy, perhaps.

'Peppi's a colourful person,' I said, 'but I don't think this was her crowd. They're violent. She was molested, thrown into the back of a pickup and abducted. Her neighbours haven't heard from her for – ' I hesitated, how long was it? An aching body warps time.

'I tell you, Penelope ran with a weird crowd downtown. Even at high school she dug up some dillies. At seventeen years old she was acting in Central Park in New York. Shakespeare, Tennessee Williams, Eugene O'Neill, the whole lot of 'em.'

Her citation of three literary giants seemed out of joint, but cheered me slightly. I prodded her on.

'Peppi has a magnificent voice, fine delivery.'

Mrs Maronek's glasses flashed.

'You seen her act?'

'Not on stage.'

'She blew a career all right. They don't have nobody like her. Why, when she was seven, eight years old she could recite "Robert Service". Went on for twenty minutes.'

'You never thought of putting her in movies, then?'

'Stuck in the back end of Honolulu? Sure! Anyways, Penelope wasn't the kind of kid you could sell margarine with. She wouldn't lay down, not her!'

'You were living in Hawaii?'

Mrs Maronek examined me. Suspended behind a plume of cigaret smoke, her square, leathery face, mopped hair and pink-rimmed glasses resembled a ritual mask. In bizarre sympathy, the luridly painted children wept on in the background.

'Why you wanna know, mister?'

My assumptions about the maternal link had taken a beating. Maybe professionals get hard-boiled about such things, but as an emotionally involved amateur I still didn't want to give up the idea that a woman would want to help me find her daughter.

'Mrs Maronek, your daughter – my friend, and the girl that I asked to . . . ' I started again. 'Obviously you mentioning you once lived in Honolulu makes me think that – well, you made enemies, I mean I'm groping. The police are no use, they escorted me off the island. I'm a complete stranger to you, I realize, but me and Peppi are going to . . . when we get back together . . . '

I didn't like it, but I couldn't help it. The emotion and the frustration were real and so were the tears, but they were being exposed in a hostile environment with no prospect of comfort. The baleful mask puffed fumes and glinted as I floundered around in confusion, wiping my eyes off clumsily with my coat sleeve.

When control returned, the black velours tears welling up out of kitsch children were a mockery . . .

Still the artist didn't budge.

It occurred to me that Peppi hated her mother. Had killed her, rebuilt her in a foreign land. At the same time my body tightened, preparing to get up, make excuses, get out.

But my heart hung on. Dogged things, hearts.

'I get a weird impression,' I said, sniffing hard and swallowing, 'you don't give a goddamn what's happened to Peppi. I guess I should get the hell out of here. Just tell me one thing. Suppose Peppi had been kidnapped. Can you think of any reason why?'

The cigaret smoke arced upwards, flared, and the drab mouth uttered in thick smoke: 'Gangbang?'

The weeping children stared at me pleadingly. I had harboured the same suspicion. It was more than I could bear. All the same, Lieutenant Lau didn't fit in to the picture. More had to be revealed to Mrs Maronek, who had readjusted herself into a posture of lewd invitation, her décolletage, a parody version of Peppi's, arrayed in front of her across a bolster.

'Truth is,' I said, 'I thought so too. The gang involved were capable of it. I went after them figuring that was the score.'

A pang of mistrust brought me up. The woman in front of me who said she was Peppi's mother had lived in Honolulu with Peppi as a kid. Lau lived in Honolulu. I didn't like Lau. I didn't like the woman. Yet the more I sensed a connection, the more I needed a lead.

'Something happen to change your mind?' Mrs Maronek inquired.

'Yes, I crashed my car looking for them. When I woke up, four days later, the Honolulu Police Department told me I'd driven into a military installation and was under suspicion of spying.'

'They got a lot o' military installations over there. One whole island is a bomb target. Maybe you did stray into military territory. They're jumpy about them kind of things.'

'These guys were so jumpy they shipped me out of town the day I came to.'

'Yeah. You look banged up. I noticed that.' She sucked on her butt and stubbed it out in a brass basin impassively. A Maytag commercial started playing.

I said: 'How come I went looking for Peppi and ended up getting run out of town by the Police Department?'

'Maybe she doesn't like you.'

I stood up, said something about not getting anywhere and made for the plate-glass door. It had no handle. She came up behind me and I caught a whiff of a lazy smell that mingled heavy perfume with unwelcome implications. It was one avenue of information nothing would persuade me to explore. Turning to face her, I said: 'How come Peppi's name is Harman and yours is Maronek? What happened to her father?'

She took off her glasses and sized me up with a knowing little smile, like a lothario eyeing pussy. Hard to tell what she'd done to herself, but maybe once she'd been a good-looker. As it was, I felt like butcher's meat on a hook.

'He moved downhill to better things,' she said, and the line sounded as if it had been etched smooth by plenty of acid feeling. She added hopefully: 'But he's got trouble now.'

'So's Peppi,' I said.

'She ain't bad.'

It seemed like the first real thing Peppi's mother had let slip. I squared up. 'Then tell me if you have any idea what's happening to her.'

She was shaking her head, a sphinx again.

'I tell you one thing, Mr . . . '

'Wallace.'

' . . . Penelope can look after herself. You don't need to go snoutin' around like a horny bloodhound. Ha, ha!'

With that she apparently abandoned her designs on me. The

door slid open, I shrugged and walked out, to find night falling. Through Mrs Maronek's tinted windows you couldn't tell. I turned, but she was already a blur behind the glass. Then the porch light cut out.

I walked to my car, looked up into the California stars and said: 'Penelope.'

12

NO answer came from above, which looked depressingly big and successful. The bigger it looked, the further away all lifeguards seemed.

I sat in the Jaguar with high-tension cables twisted round my stomach. Night came down as though it was my fault.

A couple of sleek tinted-window sedans like hearses scrunched onto drives and nosed into self-opening garages, their commuter pilots docking into hidden armchairs equipped with highballs and evening news-screens. Even the trees and shrubs looked like children neglected by corporate-climbing mothers. No vehicle suggesting Hedwig R. Maronek arrived to fill the space beside the murky Toyota atop the ramp across the way. My despondency and indecision gradually evolved into a surveillance.

A late-model Mercedes swung into a drive on my side of the road, the garage doors pivoting up to reveal an inner threshold and a warm domestic interior perfect for two consumers, one-and-a-half children and a piece of a dog. It was a place for people who wanted to arrive somewhere. My idea with Peppi was to go places. I checked the glove box for cigarets, but it was no good: I'd given them up when Laurie died of cancer.

Suddenly a big collector's Caddie in cream and coffee, the type with a spare-wheel moulding on the trunk and a weeny oval back window, banged against the steep Maronek drive, swayed up the slope and screeched to a halt in the carport as a remote-control light switched on, illumining the ceiling and my nerves.

A business suit with a powerfully built man inside it got out, complete with briefcase, dark-rimmed glasses and sawn-off semibald brain. It was all I saw before he crossed the carport behind the Toyota and entered the house. Then the neighbourhood stopped screaming at me and died again. The light went out.

Blood hisses in your head, movement is effortless, thought goes one-track: prowling is good for the heart. I spirited myself all-powerfully up the drive to find the Caddie driverside door unlocked. The flashlight I'd brought from my car showed bare seats, empty footwells, no documents. There was silence. A loud click broke it.

A second or two passed and I realized the sound came from a hot engine block cooling but by then I was already stooping behind a group of plastic garbage cans, which was lucky because the door the business suit had entered reopened and the light went back on.

The Maronek woman's voice, more like a high-pitched man's, was miffed and whiney.

'Fer Chrissake Heddie, she's hot-doggin' around with some more of those crazy actor bums. She'll show.'

Maronek's voice suited his frame, heavy and brutish.

'He shoulda bin locked up by now.'

'There's no way he could get it together.'

'Leaning on him was a damn-fool idea, we should've done it my way.'

The Caddie door opened. They were eight feet away.

'She took off to New York and I never saw her for eight months. Her own mother. What makes you think this is any diff'rent?'

He replied like a man who rarely got rattled and got doubly rattled when he did.

'That was ten years ago, and anyway, she despised you.' He made it sound like Peppi had a point.

'So where're you taking off to now?'

'Gotta see a guy about this, he's in LA tomorrow.'

The way her tone changed suggested she had other ideas. I wondered if she was giving off the smell.

'Call them, Heddie. Stay in tonight.'

'Lay off. This kinda business I don't do with a call.'

The door clunked, the starter clashed and with a hissing mill and screeching tires Mr Maronek flew the roost.

The woman took only a second or two to go back in. I moved forward to follow her, but when the light went off curiosity tugged me on tiptoe down the drive and across the street to the Jaguar, which pointed after Maronek.

You don't see the 50s Caddies much any more, which made Maronek's back end more distinctive, but the suburban heights curved like dollar signs and for five minutes I thought I'd lost him.

After ten minutes I realized I had.

Mrs Maronek grunted when the door slid past my face. She was holding a paintbrush and had on a smock smeared with radioactive colours. In a preoccupied way she turned her back and let me follow her downstairs into a sectioned-off basement studio where she created her works by the light of two gro-lux neon tubes. Under the violet light there were rolls of velours, slobbering cans of paint, jars of spattered brushes, a strong whiff of acetone and a Mexican orphan (you could tell by the sombrero) sprouting a globule at each eye. The peasant blouse glowed uncannily white in the UV effect. Mrs Maronek laid a baton across the picture, rested her brush hand on it, and dabbed at the eye as if she were alone.

I went round and faced her from beside the picture. Her glasses were rearing against the violet smoke coming from her stogy.

'Something smells bad.'

'You been watching my place?'

'I want Peppi back. You'd better cut loose.'

The dull stare.

'Or what?'

I moved a pace forward, pushing a wall of bad air towards her.

'How come your old man skedaddled when you told him about Peppi being snatched?'

More dull stare. Then she coughed and hacked her guts out,

dropping the stub end onto the floor in a tress of spittle. She shrugged.

'Don't get all riled up. We reckoned Pete Harman might've gone and done somethin' stupid, that's all.'

'Harman? Is that her father?'

Mrs Maronek threw her tools aside. She'd plateaued on booze and uppers and looked relieved to abandon her sickly work. She sank against a stool and lit another cigaret and spoke a weir of violet vapour.

'Pete Harman, non-Pulitzer-prizewinner, nontalent, non-person.'

The definition came smoothly, like a series of well-worn worry beads.

'I fell in love with him in 'fifty-nine down in Acapulco,' she said. 'You could rent a hammock on the beach for ten cents a night in those days. He was bumming round writing the great novel of the century and soaking up a lot of mescal and tequila for ideas. I had the use of a villa at the time and spent my time painting the scenery. Heh! Seen better days, ain't I.'

She sniffed, caught smoke in her nose and choked.

'Anyways, he kinda moved onto my scene, moved into my house and pretty soon moved into me, not that he was much to write home about that way, with the booze. Still, I thought he was a genius. I'd never seen anybody drink like he did.'

She picked up a lowball from beside the easel and gulped a big hit.

'He'd go for months without knowing what day it was, what time it was, nothin', just sitting on the stoop mouthing off at the sea or shut away with his beat-up typewriter. Used to take off and dry out somewhere up the coast for a month or two then come back with a few bucks and take up where he left off. That's how he kept going. I had Peppi, but he hardly noticed. We took a shot at making out stateside, New Mexico, Honolulu, LA, but his head went off like a bad egg. The great quotations came out jumbled up. He smashed typewriters. One time he pitched one out the apartment window and damn near killed the neighbour's kid on the sidewalk.'

'Fatal charm,' I said.

She ignored me, intent on counting off her bitterness beads.

'One day he drove from our place in Long Beach up to see some guru guy in Hollywood – you can bet he was a deadbeat – and he came halfway back down the Santa Monica freeway on the wrong side of the divider. Got the best part of five miles before the highway patrol picked him up. Been in and out of hospital ever since. They fix him up a bit, put him to work in one of those bakeries or some such halfway help joint, but he's on the dope sooner or later and they shut him up again.'

She emptied the glass, and half filled it with neat vodka.

'He still reckons he has a family, though.'

'I guess. Yep.'

She glowered at her ash-drooping butt and crammed it into a plate of mouldy food scraps.

'And you reckon he could've pulled this thing with Peppi? Why?'

'Don't underestimate him,' she came back sharply, slurring a little. 'I told you, Pete Harman has lucid patches. He's no genius, but he's cunning. Learned it in the institutions . . . Anyway,' she added, giving me a covert glance half blocked by the rim of her glasses, 'he's got dough. His mother just died.'

'The insane can't inherit,' I objected.

Another queer glance.

'I never had him committed,' she blurted, faltering. 'I never had the guts. We had something going . . . once.'

Emotion sounded mawkish in Mrs Maronek, as if her eyes might start bulging and come up with a single golfball-size tear. She fumbled another cigaret alight.

'You don't think he's taken Peppi somewhere.'

All I could see was her tangled hair as she sucked.

'I hope he didn't. I'm not saying he couldn't have, I just hope he didn't. He could get locked up for ever this time. HR's worried. He thinks Pete might've gone nuts and grabbed Penelope with some crazy theory about looking after her.'

It was a generous version of his reaction in the garage.

'Where's your husband gone?'

She didn't answer straight away. Subtly, the ground shifted. The bad air pushed back towards me as she sniffed and straightened up.

'I don't know,' she decided to say. 'I have nothing to do with his work. He thinks he may be able to find out something. He has a lot of . . . people.'

'What is your husband's work, Mrs Maronek?'

Another pause.

''S a security consultant.'

The electric front door slid across my mind.

'Have you called Harman?'

The menace shifted away. She seemed to be withdrawing, turning into another piece of studio art junk.

'I've never called him. He's a nonnumber.'

She was gathering herself into a little poisonous pearl of hate. I almost shouted across the gulf: 'Where can I check him out? Where did you last hear of him?'

'Far away,' she said, as if she'd already gone after him. 'Compton County Hospital in LA. They got a garbage dump there. He should be on it. Who knows, maybe he won a trip to Hawaii in a needle-threading competition.'

'I'll see what I can do,' I said, making for the stairs.

'You go down there, you go down there, you go down there,' she went like a stuck record behind me. She worked the door and I left her to pop a goofball and get back on track.

The Redwood City lights looked good. Another earthquake would have.

13

I TOOK hold of the car door handle intending to drive to San Francisco International and ride a shuttle to LA to see Pete Harman. Maybe he still had contacts on the island he'd once inhabited. Apparently he had money: maybe it could do some talking. But it was hard to concentrate while something was heaping iron bars onto my shoulders.

Opening the door and getting in behind the wheel was like paid work. Eyesight blurred, side aching, nerves bejangled, I sat gripping the wheel of the stationary car and listening to the feedback squawks in my synapses. A sure and commanding power was arising to terminate activity in the alarmed organism called Wallace. The elastic connection which stretched all the way to University Hospital, Honolulu, was about to snap under a force of unconquerable hunger and thirst and injury and fatigue.

Somehow I got home. A long recorded live session by Art Pepper on FM ... me on automatic pilot ... my mind on Peppi in a place in outer space where there was smooth green grass and a rippling stream.

A mile before Santa Flora, Peppi turned into a refrigerator. My refrigerator. And I drove for it the way a man with dysentery makes for the john.

Nothing registered until I was standing in the kitchen, lighted only by the open fridge, glugging back a quart of UHT milk, which I followed with a slab of Emmenthal cheese on Swedish crispbread, four cold boiled potatoes well salted, two bananas deep-throated, and a pint tub of live yogurt well past its sell-by date. There remained half an onion going mouldy and an open can of tomato sauce, but I passed them over and stumbled through the furnishings of my life intent on only one object, the spongy and horizontal one, which I flopped onto while in the act of removing my huarachos. One of them came off before consciousness pulled the plug.

Sharp pressure in the bladder delivered me to dawn, and after relieving it I could remember who I was, so I took myself into the shower, gave me a wash, and got myself dressed in some clean clothes. Fresh-perked Mocha Brazil nerved me up ready for the answerphone.

The answerphone was ready back. No messages.

Information helped me get in touch with several hospitals in the Compton area of Los Angeles, and at one of them they confirmed that Mr Peter Harman was a patient, and that he could be visited at any reasonable hour. There was no need to book a flight, so I took the Subaru back to San Francisco International.

By LA standards it was not a long taxi ride to Compton from the airport, only thirty minutes of dawdling noon tailback. I was delivered to a group of cheap stucco buildings of five or six storeys which could have been a welfare housing estate, downmarket office complex or an army barracks. Only a sign at the edge of the ragged lawns saying THE COMPTON COUNTY HOSPITAL INSTITUTE convinced me the address was right.

The reception area had foggy windows and scrawny naugahyde furniture. A desk clerk with a plastic smile gestured me to make myself comfortable while she called a doctor. I got the impression from her apologetic fussing that visitors were rare.

After five minutes a brunette in her early thirties approached, clicking along the vinyl corridor on steel-tipped talons. Her white ward coat was open, revealing a white blouse, cut severely but made of a silky fabric, and garlanded with an ivory-butted stethoscope. Her skirt was darkest midnight, like her net stockings and glossy shoes. There was an expression of controlled apprehension on her brainy, taut, semipretty face. Elegant of bone, with her hair mantillaed into a bun, she seemed like a character parachuted in from another set. I stood up.

'Please do sit down and relax, Mr Wallace,' she opened competently. 'My name is Dr Petreen.'

'Thanks.' I lowered my butt onto battered naugahyde, she took a cane armchair, and we squared up. She had nice green eyes which were rendered fierce as a hawk's by a strabismus which, when it found its range, conveyed a psychic jolt, compelling me to avert my gaze past her ear. I looked down the daunting perspective of the institutional corridor and felt a mental lurching, as if it would take not long in this place to turn from visitor into inmate.

The doctor tucked her clipboard into her lap, leaning forward and joining the pads of her fingers. Her skirt stretched back to reveal her gauzy black knees, which were smooth and featureless.

'Pete's been with us at Compton for a very long time,' she said in a diplomatic way that with a sinking heart I interpreted as: he's a basket case.

'But he's not a certified patient,' I countered hopefully.

The doctor raised delicately marked eyebrows. 'Oh no, Pete is quite free to come and go. After ten years in and out he's attained rather a celebrity status, particularly with our creative writing department. We still hope for great things.' She smiled and bit her lip.

'Is Pete, uh . . . all right?' I asked.

'Why yes, perfectly,' she retorted airily. After a pause, perhaps sensing an overstatement, she added: 'Actually I have only been one of his ward physicians for a comparatively short time and I'm keen to get to know his visitors.'

'Does he have any?'

'Just recently, yes.' Dr Petreen leaned forward further, unsheathing a centimetre of packaged thigh. 'And what is your connection with Pete Harman, Mr Wallace?'

There it was, out on the table, like the guts out of a fish. I was being screened. It made sense. In their way, they were doing their job. But owning people jarred with something hard in me.

I talked loosely about Peppi Harman's disappearance, letting on that I knew her so well I was about as good as family with the Harman clan.

She heard me out alertly and said: 'I don't know how much help Pete will be. He has had so little contact with his family. Now you mention it, I do remember that a daughter is listed in his file. Still, you may talk with him if you wish.'

She escorted me out of the building across a courtyard laid to patchy lawn. I accosted her by the arm halfway.

'Dr Petreen, before talking to Pete, I'd like to know more about his illness.'

When she turned to speak, the cross-eyed gimlet look was gone. It was apparently one of her tricks. I noticed she smelt of something rare, and her teeth were like a bracelet.

'What exactly worries you?'

'Well, firstly, whatever's wrong with him, it seems strange that he's been a patient here for so long, but is still not formally certified insane.'

'He's a voluntary patient, Mr Wallace. He's been rehabilitated constantly, but he keeps finding himself back here. What can I say?'

'What form does his mental illness take?'

She sniffed delicately. 'It's hard to label a patient like him. If he stays here much longer we may have to call a condition after him and list his particular package of neuroses under it.'

'Such as?'

The eyes remained in parallel and gave me a deep, unsettlingly candid scan.

'Put it this way, he is schizophrenic, but nobody has yet quite pinned down what that means. We have a professional grammar of symptoms, but it's imperfect. Only three weeks are allowed for so-called normal grief, for example. Establishment ideas of normalcy are so arbitrary and finally restrictive.'

'What kind of symptoms?' I persevered.

She reflected in a bored fashion. 'Attempted homicide? Prolonged acute depression? Among others.'

'Homicide?' I echoed. 'And you let him come and go?'

'Perfectly routine,' Petreen replied. 'The episode in question occurred a long time ago and there were no criminal charges. A prison sentence would have been a lot shorter than the time he has spent here.' The observation prompted her to glance at her wristwatch. 'Believe me, he belongs in an asylum,' she finished, leading me without further discussion across the courtyard, through another block, across more lawns where a jumbo jet threw its shadow and its thrust-roar over us and up to another identical oyster-coloured block with metal-framed windows and grimy, haphazard Venetian blinds.

After some security business at the entrance, we reached a spacious lounge which had a big stone fireplace at the far end of a bare parquet floor, some potted plants and various pieces of the kind of institutional furniture I had sat on at reception. There were two white-haired ladies occupied with handiwork near the fireplace. A younger, overweight man with rolls in his neck sat with his back to us reading. There was the characterless feel of a public waiting room in a government building which, it struck me, was exactly what it was. A tall, ginger-haired man sat erect in an armchair reading a dog-eared paperback. He looked up with a bright-blue regard that I instantly recognized.

'Here's a visitor, Pete. This is Mr Wallace. I have some papers to attend to, I shall be just next door in the duty office.' Petreen's high heels clicked away and left me alone with Peppi's father.

As he stood up, thrusting his big-boned hands into loose pant pockets, I confirmed the make: the height, the posture, the apricot hair, the classical nose. About fifty, with a balding brow that exposed freckles which showered down his masculine version of Peppi's face, he had a comb sticking out of his white cotton shirt, and his leather shoes were lacking strings. The identification was almost denied by his manner. He gave the rumpled, passive impression of a passenger on a train which had lost its way on a journey lasting many seasons, and the mouth was thin and jagged, like a portrait painter's mistake.

We sat down and I told him what had happened to Peppi. When I finished he was grasping the armrests as if to steady himself, and wearing a leery, askance expression that struck me as assumed.

As if picking up on my thought, Harman said: 'Acting's all wrong for a girl. They should use boys, like the Elizabethans, like Shakespeare, Marlowe, Jonson. It seemed inadvisable to them for a young woman to be subjected to the madness of theatre.'

He used a restrained, professorial tone which came out as if it had been typed on his brain for reproduction in voice. The accent was cultivated, almost English, of the sort affected by 1930s Hollywood matinee stars. It clashed with his dress, but revealed a man with an unpredictable inner dimension. News of Peppi's disappearance seemed to provoke him no more than it had his ex-wife.

'Why did Peppi go to Hawaii, Mr Harman?'

He frowned, as if casting his mind back decades. 'I haven't seen her for years.'

'She seems to have had a good job at a college in Palo Alto.'

'Uh-huh,' he nodded, as if humouring me.

'Why take off and work on a quiet beach at the back end of Oahu?'

He clicked his tongue and shook his head.

'Did she ever tell you what was on her mind?'

He clawed his hair.

'Did she get into trouble at college?'

Trouble seemed to snag his attention, as it had his estranged wife's. He gave me a different look, as though the real man peered out from behind the patient's mask, suspicious, but interested.

'Who are you?' he asked, fair and square. The question surprised me, coming from a man in his predicament, but it seemed to indicate progress.

'I write about architecture,' I told him. 'Currently I'm putting together a picture book called *The Stick Style*. It's about the kind of houses we don't put up any more because we've got too much money and too little time. I was picture-searching in Hawaii, met Peppi and we decided on the spot to get married.' I paused to check that he was receiving me. 'We'll be in-laws,' I added tentatively.

'You divorced?' he asked.

'No, I'm a widower. My wife died of cancer five years ago.'

'Kids?'

'Nope.'

He put the next question lightly, with a slight roll of the eye, as if I might object. 'What was her name?'

'Laura. Why do you ask?'

He wagged an index finger. 'Her full name. Full maiden name, the one she was born into.'

'Laura Fenella Kramer.'

'Laura Kramer,' he repeated dreamily, fiddling with the tips of his fingers and gazing past me.

I waited, wondering what was so compelling about this man who felt at home in an emotional railroad-station waiting room. Petreen had mentioned him being something of a celebrity among the doctors. Could he have found on a schizophrenic ward a bizarre fulfilment of his career? Here he had both an audience for his writerly ideas and a sort of vocation: full-time lunatic. It could beat working.

Harman's fingers stopped and he fixed a gaze on my brow so intense that you might have thought there was a beautiful view through it.

'Your wife was an angel,' he muttered, narrowing his eyes.

I waved the compliment away. His channelling act did not hold much fascination.

'Shucks, she was a great pal and a beautiful woman, but – '

'The vast prolixity of life is such,' he interrupted, 'that calculation has become harder, but there is no doubt in the evidence of your wife's name that she was one of the angelic host. Indeed, she could have lived no longer than she did. Angels are taken up at roughly three-thousand-two-hundred-and-eighty-five days – you have to allow for leap years and other variables – six-thousand-five-hundred-and-seventy days and nine-thousand-eight-hundred-and-fifty-five days. I assume your wife was twenty-seven years old at her decease?'

'Well,' I groped, 'yes, she was.'

'Of course she was, no other conclusion possible,' Harman said, as if he had demonstrated a theorem to a stumbling student. 'Angelhood is an unusual gift, but still far more common than most people realize.'

'This is getting way off the point,' I came back. 'Do you know people in Hawaii who could help me get in touch with Peppi? You don't seem to understand, I've been thrown out of the state. I'm looking for – help . . . '

I trailed off. Harman had pursed his lips and turned to look out the window, where past shabby eucalyptus trees you could see an elevated freeway in the haze.

It was the end of the interview. Peter Harman would speak no more. I'd hit the wrong button on his computer and the screen had gone blank. He sat logged off, with his lips sealed, looking fixedly away into an inward perspective.

It was such an experienced cool-out, no doubt the fruit of much practice on better interrogators than I, that I quickly gave up, took my leave of Peppi's father and, with heavy heart, went in search of Dr Petreen, whom I found in a bare little office with its door open a few yards up the corridor.

She greeted me absently, squiggling signatures on documents, then tied them all away in a red ribbon and accompanied me out of the building. It felt good to get back into fresh air, even the Los Angeles version of it. There was nothing overtly disturbing about the ward – to judge by Harman's behaviour the bars were inside the patient's heads – but it was a relief to escape.

'Even though he seized up on you, what did you think?' Petreen inquired. 'Frankly none of our patients get many visitors, I'd like to know your reaction.'

'From a talk as brief as that I can't really judge,' I said. 'But I figure he's mad, all right.'

Petreen seemed to find this a vulgar remark.

'We've worked long and hard to get away from parading people like Pete Harman around in cages,' she said.

'Yes, you let him come and go as he pleases.'

'It's always conditional,' she said.

'How conditional?'

'Well, his wife has been in touch with us about him.'

'Recently?'

'Yes.'

'Since his mother's death?'

'Yes. She said she felt an inheritance changed the situation.'

'You mean, broke Pete Harman's harmless, rich he's suddenly a menace to the community.'

Her voice went frosty. 'I can't comment on that, Mr Wallace.'

I felt like grabbing her by the white linen lapels. 'Why not? Don't you see that if Harman lost his liberty his wife could control the estate?'

'And the daughter?'

'Exactly! She'd have a claim, wouldn't she?'

Dr Petreen remained very cool. 'You will have to consult an attorney about it, Mr Wallace. We're running a hospital here.'

She saw me to the entrance hall and directed me to a taxi stand nearby.

So I found myself back in the street. It didn't look any better than before. Something bright and sustaining was sinking inside me.

I looked down the road. It seemed to lead to the taxis, but I knew it led back to a violet light in Redwood City, so-called Mrs Maronek, and Mr, too. Then it occurred to me in this form: I hadn't seen Peppi for a week.

14

THE taxi took my body towards the San Diego freeway but my soul was in H. R. Maronek's garage trying to replay what had been said there the night before as I crouched behind the Toyota. It was something about 'leaning on him too hard'.

I wondered who they were leaning on. And what they were leaning on them for. I wondered about Pete Harman's inheritance. I wondered so much I started kneading my hands like a keening widow. People go weird in the backs of cabs.

A jumbo jet angled lazily up from the airport in the distance and the freeway traffic came to a halt. The fumes in the back of the cab thickened. From the raised highway there was an uninspiring panoramic view of greater LA, Inglewood, Culver City, South Gate, Downey, mostly tract housing, broken up by multistorey boxes and a scattering of downhearted palm trees. Across miles of gang-warfare territory, downtown was lost in a smog shroud on the horizon. I wondered whether Pete Harman's literary ambitions had added up to anything.

I was getting the shakes. There's no good place for it; the back of a cab jammed on an LA freeway is the worst. A huge dose of futility had been injected into me. I'd caught a dose of depression off the hospital furniture. I was running out of fight. I threw a bill at the driver, got out of the cab and blundered through the fumes to the rim of the freeway deck.

Let No Man Put Asunder

Two hours later I was still walking. Not fast, not slow. Taking in nothing. If a cop had asked my name I would have had to check my driver's licence. I stopped somewhere for a burger. The world went by, the burger went down, gave me heartburn. The misty, easy-over LA sun passed across the sky until it was shining weakly up the boulevard over my shoulder onto the looming black eighty-storey totem poles of downtown and making them glint nastily. More time passed. I accepted a ride. Somebody told me I was in a precinct called Canoga Park. They assured me it was part of the City of Los Angeles.

My legs ached: I got on a bus. Soon a headache started. I was sitting on the back bench, where the engine laboured hardest, among the people who ride buses in LA, city of six million automobiles. City of the Hollywood Freeway, world's densest car drain. City second only to Detroit in making four-wheeled hair dryers.

There was a brown-skinned high-school student, a man with a hat which looked like a problem, a woman with a half-ton carton of detergent across her lap. Los Angeles losers. A lady joined me, white soiled raincoat, yellow and gray hair. Wrinkled face rouged. She held in her hand an ancient miniature radio which had stopped working long ago. Now it was her mike on some private intergalactic journey. She lifted it to her jaw and gave a drawling psychological report on the world. I listened, but it threw no light on my condition. Her light had gone out. After a while, she got off.

We were on Ventura Boulevard, heading west. At a stop the driver left his seat and collected tickets. I said I did not have one. He ignored me, a deeply resigned man, a shepherd of autoless souls and probably brokenhearted. He drove on, stopping, starting, grinding, slowing, halting, jerking. Ventura went on for ever. We cornered into hinterland suburbia, outer circle of unpaid maintenance, bulimia, video sex, body building, slow decay and rapid despair, where we pirouetted for an endless hour.

By the time we got back onto Hollywood Boulevard I was punchy with anonymous bus riders, so many people had got on and off, only me staying on the back bench – me and the brokenhearted ferryman up front. I was a white man flanked by two black men: Uncle-Tom black men who rode buses through crackland. There was a pasty-faced guy sitting across from me in pink, orange and yellow duds with stains. He was puffily overweight, had black dark glasses on, and a soiled bandage-cum-bandanna tying his cranium together. He had a two-foot-long transistor radio bound onto his arm with dirty adhesive tape: he apparently lived, ate and slept this way. The radio was not playing – he was. He bopped, he boogied, he delivered the news, he hosted a phone-in program and supplied the guests, all in brain-damaged nonsense out of a slobbery, unformed mouth. I felt like leaning over and twisting his ear to retune his head. Did all roads round here lead to Compton? I gazed out the window at passing palm trees. We were on Vine, passing the Capitol building.

My head was too hurtful and I was too despondent for drink. I took another bus, which let me out onto Santa Monica where it most resembles a great European boulevard, at a time when I least resembled a human being. Before me stood one of the main branches of P. K. Rayner, a flag-waving stack of coffee-coloured bricks and chocolate glazing which inspired me to make for the drugs department and buy a lot of pain-killer.

The diesel engine had loosened the rivets in my legs. It seemed like a twenty minute routemarch across the parking lot. Only losers walked any more. Thousands of losers had ambled, shoved, glided past me in the last few hours; all sorts, all races, all shapes and sizes and varieties of gender; I'd heard a jabber of foreign lingos, and strings of nonsense in my own. I had taken a trip in the armpit of America and the last thing I expected was to recognize anyone in a parking lot twice the size of a football field.

She was prettier than I recalled, with a cuter figure and a splayed-out, dancerly gait. She looked a lot more like a flight attendant or a manicurist or an ad agency receptionist than a shrink. I strained to remember her name, and failed. The one person I knew!

I ambled after her into P. K. Rayner. The odour of perfume, fabric, hairspray and massed femalehood hit me in the gut. For a moment my vision blurred. I concentrated on following the figure in the two-piece loose gray costume with her hair bobbed prettily on top of her head, the little neck all bare and tender, the medium heels of the size-tiny shoes going tip-tap on the parquet aisles.

She went to the wall and placed her hand against it, looking up at an indicator. She tapped her pert toe, took a compact out of her soft leather shoulder bag and checked her eyes. I heard it click shut; she put it away. She checked the indicator again. She looked at the ground. She looked up sharply once more. Through my fog I got a notion that this was one gal who was not going shopping. She shifted her weight around, flouncing her hips, and turned towards me.

Desk calendars in imitation crocodile and mock gold suddenly transfixed my attention as she passed. I caught a whiff of her. It was rustling silk, powdered naked skin, wheatfields, oatmeal, violets. I followed the trail, like a trapper tracking a spoor of discarded underclothes. Strange things happen to men in department stores. But at least my senses were clearer. And the sharper my intuition became, the less anything made sense, but I kept going.

We rode the moving staircase, twenty steps apart. She got to the next flight early enough to look down at me, but she kept on looking up: nobody looks down escalators.

We kept going that way, her getting off a few steps after I got on, past the drugstore – it was on floor three, demarcated by dividers and a big sign reading ELEPHANT DRUGS – as far as floor six, the top floor for shoppers. She headed through a golf department, saunas and sauna accessories, coffee shop, past a savings-and-loan counter, an accounts and credit-card counter and an inquiry desk, which was where she stopped.

The credit-card application brochure at the accounts department could have been written in Serbo-Croat. All I knew was, her conversation with the inquiry lady was inaudible. I could hear the voices, I could pick up the nuances, but there was a lot of action with the afternoon coffee-time crockery across the way and the pair I wanted to hear might as well have been blowing raspberries at each other. I could read one thing, though: my ladyfriend had pressing business with someone on the penthouse storey. Before I could peruse the back of my application she had been admitted to the inner sanctum via a heavy-looking walnut-grained door discreetly set into the panelling beside the inquiry counter.

There was a ballpoint chained to a disc. I picked it up and wrote in the Name of Applicant box (Capital Letters Only Please): DR PETREEN, and handed it to CAREY, ASSISTANT CREDIT MANAGER with a grin, chucking her under the badge. She was a big girl, with a big face and a big blush.

'Would you by any chance have any paracetamol handy, Carey?'

I took Carey's five tablets towards the smell of coffee coming from The Hacienda Room, where I carried three apple danish and two steaming mugs to a ketchup-smeared plastic table under a foam-wood pergola and made a refreshing snack.

The sugary pastries energized me, the coffee stimulated my nerves and the tablets sent the brain disease away. Strands of the day came together round the heavily stressed hole in the middle of it and started to form a scar. It occurred to me as I watched the tall curly-haired black girl working the cash register for a skinny Arab-looking dude in a djellaba that I was still spending the cash I had withdrawn at the savings bank branch in Wahiawa. Too much had happened, too quickly.

I rode quietly down the silver staircases in a shaft of chrome and smoked glass to the ground floor and sought out the perfume counter nearest the elevator doors. There were many fragrances to sample. I got into them with the petite Jewish sales lady, who thought I was cute to be taking such care.

There was an authentic purchase of 100 ml of Femme de Rochas going down when the elevator doors opened and revealed a Dr Petreen turned ghastly, her hair unpinned and falling tangled over a bleached, mortified face, flanked by two uniformed security guards who steered her briskly towards the nearest exit.

I stuffed the box into my coat pocket and made after them. The dicks' heads and shoulders among the parked cars twenty yards away showed they were standing over her, one holding the door, the other as backup, as she got into her car. No doubt about it, the lady was being seen off the property.

It was a cream Alfetta, in prime condition. The guards gaped across the roof as I greeted them, opened the passenger door and slung myself in.

15

'HOME, James,' I said. She glared only long enough to identify me and went back to getting out of there. The engine uttered a nervy, elastic whine and we were propelled forward in an arc towards P. K. Rayner to grab the main feeder aisle to the boulevard. As we lurched around, a blurry sky-blue-suited figure veered into our route, teetering on pointy heels, arms flailing. We squealed to a halt and I tried out the strength of the windshield with a sharp crack of the upper left temple.

My driver cranked the window down but kept looking at me, not out at the confused, apologetic saleslady holding out my change. Dr Petreen's expression was hostile, harassed, end-of-tether and dried-up-tearstains, but just a bit amazed.

I reached past her expression for the money as it was handed in through the window.

'Drive on,' I said. Wordlessly, she obeyed.

She took it all out on the commuter traffic, darting, weaving, skidding, burning rubber until we were doing a decent speed in the outside lane of the expressway headed south. She drove straight-armed, with her chin rammed into her chest, occasionally clawing the hair off her face. Then we came to a tailback where there was no escape. We jerked to a halt and she slumped forward pressing her forehead on the wooden wheel rim and rocking it from side to side. I wondered if you had to be crazy to work at Compton or whether it just helped.

'You giving me a ride back to the hospital?'

'Never going to that shithole again,' she muttered.

'Can you drop me as near as you're going, then?' No reply. I added: 'I think Pete Harman may be in danger.'

'Nothing could hurt him,' she snarled. 'He has no feelings. He's cra-a-a-zy.' She cooed the word out on a disturbing note.

'I think his wife knew about Peppi Harman's abduction before I told her about it yesterday.'

The ravaged little face came up with a weal across the brow. She surveyed the seething, shimmering mass of steel and glass ahead as if it were a whirlpool into which she was being sucked.

'What happened back there?' I asked. 'Were you caught shoplifting in the executive suite?'

She kept glaring ahead. After a tremulous minute, she drew a jerky breath.

'I just resigned from Compton Hospital,' she said. 'In fact I just resigned from the medical profession. And from the human race.' She kept looking ahead. 'So I guess I can talk about Pete Harman.' She looked at me with firework eyes. 'What d'you want to know?'

The traffic ahead moved. We eased forward in our turn, like a freight wagon.

'Harman's inheritance. How much is involved?'

'Everything is involved, including his sanity,' she said. 'He's been a poor little rich boy all his adult life. Nothing chews a man up worse than that. If you mean how much money is involved, it's plenty.'

'How plenty?'

'Ten, fifteen million in cash and stocks. The same again tied up in land and long-term bonds.'

'How d'you know?'

'Pete told me.'

'But he's insane.'

'Partly,' she answered. 'So is the whole planet.'

I let that go. It seemed to sum up Compton's problem. 'Why was Harman so poor when his family was so rich?'

'He wanted to know, too. His major problem was his mother.' She snorted. 'What else is new with men?'

'Oedipal?' I said.

'More Hamletian. Pete's convinced that his father was a

scientific genius and that his mother was a suburban slob who made a brilliant man waste his talents on commerce. And then she heaped insult on betrayal by parlaying the assets into multi-millions after driving the old man into an early grave.'

'And starving her son.'

'He was already highly strung. She wound him up and snapped him.'

'Who did he try to kill?'

'His wife, fifteen years ago. He went berserk and smashed their place up.'

I thought of the Maronek woman's face and tried to match it with a severe battering: it fitted.

'I gather he liked to drink.'

'Tests proved he was stone-cold sober. He was on a religious kick. It was ironic: he'd even published a book on the Sacred Path of Peace or some such thing. It was the nearest he'd ever been to getting recognition, and he blew it.'

'Did he go to jail?'

'She refused to lay charges. He was guilty. He went to the neighbours with blood all over his shirt. When they shut the door in his face he walked to the local radio station and turned himself in. The whole episode was too irrational for the courts to handle. He agreed to become a psychiatric outpatient.'

'And so launched his career.'

'Huh?'

'Forget it. What kind of relationship does he have with Peppi?'

Dr Petreen cast me a keen, parallax look. 'If he abused her, he kept the secret through a hundred group therapy sessions.'

'That kind of stuff can be buried deep.'

Something like a blush warmed her face, and she arched an eyebrow contemptuously. You could see the streak of guts that had got her where she was – or wasn't any more, I couldn't be sure.

'You're running pretty deep yourself, mister boyfriend. You think your chum disappearing may have something to do with Peter Harman's fortune? Is that it?'

'Peppi's his child. Her mother doesn't give a damn about her.'

Dr Petreen removed her hands from the wheel and clapped them to her temples (we were moving at a crawl).

'What a day,' she moaned. 'Now it's infanticide.'

I said: 'I don't think it's murder.'

'Wait. Don't tell me. You got a feeling.'

'You're bitter,' I told her. 'Yeah, I got a feeling.'

Not true. I didn't have any feelings. I was a Peppi robot.

'Okay, I'll drop you at the hospital,' she said, and fell silent, accelerating towards an exit ramp that had opened up.

16

THE Compton mental hospital looked familiar, almost homely, after a deranged day. It was easy to imagine how the drab buildings with their steamy aroma of potatoes could turn into a haven for the study of needle threading and lower-lip drubbing. Taking a deep breath, I crossed the highway.

Not far from the taxi stand, a hobo was leaning against the window of a liquor store. He made a clicking noise at me. Cowhands on the ranch at home had used to talk to their mounts the same way, and my horsy streak pulled me up.

It was a tall, balding man with ginger hair and a cascade of freckles over his thin face, which he cocked at me. He had a rumpled white open-necked shirt on, with a comb sticking out of the breast pocket, baggy pants tied with a tortured necktie and stringless tie-up leather shoes.

'Hi, Peter,' I said easily, and moved towards him. He fitted in comfortably with the rest of my day, a day which was not far from turning into a dog-end. A shaft from its glowing embers played on the side of his face, throwing one haughty eye into deep shadow and lighting a glint there.

'Where's Penelope?' he said, keeping his hands rammed into his pockets and talking through a smouldering filterless king-size.

'I think she's being held hostage. Have you been approached about it?'

Harman lazily pulled his right hand halfway out of his pants and looked down at it. He was showing an elasticated wad of

$100 bills as thick as three decks of cards, resting against the scarred inside of his wrist. He dropped it back into the deep pocket and used the hand to knock off his cigaret, which he dragged at heavily. Cars came and went on the highway. There was nothing but the noise of them in my brain.

'You got any more o' that?' I asked.

The left arm crooked, and a second prayer book of bills deeked out of the other pocket.

'How much?' I asked, throwing good manners aside.

'Four hunnerd thou,' he said doubtfully. 'There's more on the way.'

Three Latinos in jeans and chequered shirts burst out of the liquor store and swung by us on a wave of singsong chatter and aftershave. Two black dudes in ripped denim appeared round the corner and shouldered in through the door.

'Let's talk,' I said. 'I have to go to the airport. Ride the cab with me. You'd be better off away from the street, anyway.'

Wordlessly he dropped his butt, pushed himself off the wall with a foot and accompanied me the short distance to the taxi stand.

It was the busy time for traffic, but it wasn't far from Compton to the airport. When we were installed behind tinted windows on a leatherette sofa and out of sight of the lunatic asylum, I tackled Harman head-on.

'I can save you all that money,' I said. He sat impassively beside me, pockets bulging. 'All I need is to make a few more connections between the Maroneks and Peppi. Then I'll throw law at them, hire some heavies and go in and get her out. I swear, if you pay them now, they'll only want more.'

He kept looking ahead, with his long hands twiddling beside his legs, as if playing an invisible keyboard. His head fell forward, then turned to look at me, climbing under my gaze. 'She wants to lock me up,' he said.

'She'll have a case if you're found walking around with four hundred thousand bucks in your britches.'

'She doesn't need a case,' he said.

'Why did you try to kill her in the first place?'

His head came up.

'I never did.'

'Come on, Peter. You beat her into a coma years ago. It's what's kept you under therapy ever since. That and the habit.'

His eyes gleamed.

'You mean my wife,' he said.

'Yeah.'

'I'm not referring to my wife,' he replied with precision.

'Uh-huh,' I replied, waiting for him to set me right. But he looked ahead again. The ski-jump forehead and nose were pure Peppi. 'You're referring to who?' I asked.

He replied evenly: 'Dr Petreen.'

My head started nodding before I caught it up. 'I got it,' I said, flaring up like a tract home in a bush fire. 'You live in a mental asylum and you've got a theory your doctor is plotting against you? Shit, Peter, I think that has a kind of crappy familiar ring to it.'

'I can explain,' he said reasonably, but I was well away.

'You're sitting there with two bales a hay in your pockets – ' abruptly I cut the volume, but the cabbie's mirrored face was squashed and expressionless, possibly brain dead with fumes ' – complaining about a plot against you at Compton? Hell, why don't you rent yourself a suite at a private place in Rolling Hills, or up the coast Santa Barbara way? Or San Diego! Yeah, San Diego has a nice climate, you can go paranoid in style down there, the nurses all have big boobs and the analysts are Jewish – only the best.'

Pete Harman sat patiently through my outburst. He looked out at a coffee shop built in the form of a tomato and reached forward to point it out to the cabbie. We pulled up in the forecourt and got out. He peeled a bill off one of the wads and pushed it through the window, waiting with the wad pincered in his hand while the cabbie made change.

Inside the tomato, we took a rear booth. The place had no clientele during the heavy traffic period. Coffee came, and Peter Harman placed big hands round his cup, looked me in the eye and spoke in a different, more gutsy tone, as if his words came from the heart instead of a problem head.

'This may be a surprise after my little numerology routine about angels earlier, but I've been clinically sane for quite a while.'

I looked hard at him. He seemed to have cast a skin. The wrong mouth had evened up and softened. He could have been a guy coming off duty from some demanding job, such as professional nutcase.

'Once I was insane,' he said, with his brow creasing. 'Beating Jayne was insane. Sitting beside her on the bed for five hours until the dawn came, then walking down to the radio station and offering to be interviewed.'

'Interviewed,' I echoed.

'My shirt was stiff with blood. They turned me away. I went back to the apartment. The cops were there. Said she was in a coma and on a drip. I told them I'd been made to do it by the statue of Jesus on the Catholic church opposite our place in Alhambra.

'Jayne was a medium. Started out the way people do, a bit of weejie board, dabbling in the tarot, then table-turning, plenty of table work – until she found the voices, or the voices found her. She could've been big. Used to say Penelope held her back, kept her tied down. She managed to build up a bit of a circuit anyway, used to go channelling up Topanga, a couple of places in Bel Air, down on Malibu, flew to Vegas a few times, but it never really took off. She did a radio spot up-valley, but no TV. When she came out of the coma she'd lost her powers. But she never blamed me. Wouldn't lay a complaint. Nothing.'

There was a pause. Abstract meditation music playing on the speakers was shattered by the searing hiss of something heating under a steam pipe. Woff, woff, woff, it went as the counter man swung the jug round. The silence that followed it hummed.

'Because Jesus made you do it,' I said.

He brushed away my sarcasm. 'When it happened, she was manifesting more powerfully than I'd ever seen before. Furniture was flying. There were lasers. Cold spots. Screams and howlings.' He looked past me at an ugly inner view. 'They never believed me, but it wasn't me who broke the place up. She turned into something . . . hideous.' He focused back on me with the replay lighting up his eyes. 'Her spirit was begging me to save her. Jesus shouted at me loud and clear to beat Satan down. And that's what I did. When I came round, I found my wife lying at my feet in a pool of blood. But breathing. I checked that, and made sure she was laid out on the bed. Then I waited till dawn. It was no good going to the radio station during the night, that I knew.' He gazed into his coffee, deflated.

'I agree. You were insane,' I said. The top of his head nodded. The freckles on his receding patch looked like constellations. 'So when did you wise up?'

When he looked up his eyes were brimming.

'It took a long time,' he muttered. 'First they hooked me on dope – their kinds of dope, Seconal, Nembutal, Milltown, Codeine, intravenous Valium. That was a favorite of mine, intravenous Valium; three weeks on a desert island crammed into one hour of unconsciousness and a couple more of sleep-walking. My feet started to swell. No way did booze ever get me into such bad condition. They had me zapped out for two years.' He looked out the tomato-shaped window with the years yawning into his head. On the highway the cars were glittering unpleasantly, glowing their red lights at each other and jostling like alligators in oily shallows.

'Chemical answers to a chemical problem, I think is the way they see it. Or used to,' I said, trying to sound cool and objective. You could bet several orthodoxies had come and gone at Compton. I doubted if chemicals had ever gone, though. Chemicals were part of the structure, like security doors and white linen coats.

'A gay orderly named Steve Polarski shot me up with skag in the end.' His eyes came up to mine with a little wistful smile in them, and drifted down towards my mouth. 'It was like finding a cure at last,' he said. 'A cure for all that bad shit they'd been feeding me.'

'How come you got busted if you were being supplied from inside?'

'Because I went out.' He reached past his cup to clasp his hands together. 'You've got to realize, I thought I was cured. I believed Polarski's dope was part of my treatment. I paid for it on a special private plan, sort of a toilets Blue Shield. When I was well hooked, I walked out.'

'Uh-huh.'

'The cops only want you off the streets. Back to the asylum is okay with them. Saves paperwork, gasoline, cooler bunks,

94

court time. And why should I have minded? I'd figured by then where the best place was for my medicine. I lived on top of my supply for five years. The kind of scene junkies dream about. Free bed, free books, free paper and pen, and dope on the welfare cheque. It was like I'd died and gone to heaven.' Harman took a sip of the coffee and added matter-of-factly: 'If your needles are clean and the stuff is good, heroin's a cleaner habit than booze.'

'What intervened?'

'Polarski got shot. He had a room somewhere in Glendale. The cops set it up as a gay feud. But we weren't fooled.'

'Who's we?'

'The users on the wards. Polarski's quote patients unquote. We knew the hospital pharmacy was being privatized.'

'Your connection was shot because of that?'

'It was a little while before Bush made it to the White House. Finally the Reagan effect was filtering down to Compton. Things started getting shaken up all over. The kitchen staff were fired and the management took on a catering outfit. The cleaners got the boot and they brought in a Tong Chinese contractor with slave labour from Hong Kong and Taiwan. Then, according to Polarski, they gave the pharmacy contract to Elephant Drug. Not long after, he was dead.'

'And did the junk dry up?'

He eyed me shrewdly.

'No way, just the opposite. It started coming out of the walls. The cleaning slaves were dealing it. Strictly on behalf of the boss. They hardly dared speak what little English they knew, they were too afraid of being handed over to immigration for deportation. And the supply of disposable syringes from stores didn't dry up either. She saw to that.'

'Who?'

He said precisely, with a certain relish: 'Your friend Dr Petreen.'

'She was in on the racket?'

'Had to be, from the start. She was the cost centre for our wing. It came with the job. And she was hired right around the time they did the restructuring.'

I opened my mouth to say, Harman, Forget It, Everyone

Knows You're Crazy. But the words didn't match his face or his delivery. He seemed more like an oddball loner with a streak of childlike naiveté that had led him up one of life's blind alleys.

An instinctive connection in my head made me blurt out: 'Is the money for Dr Petreen?'

He shrugged and hoisted a sardonic eyebrow.

'Her sick mother. Brain surgery.'

'Cash?'

'That's what she said.'

'You can't be serious.'

'Why not? I don't want to be locked up.'

'Christ, it's blackmail, Harman!'

'So?'

I tried to stay controlled.

'Have they mentioned Peppi to you? Has anyone tried to – ransom her?'

'No. I've had a few letters. Couple from an Aids foundation.'

My brain chased frantically around for a link between this hospital dope racket, Petreen's extortion game and Peppi's disappearance.

'This outfit that controls the pharmacy, the one that opened the dope taps, what's it called?'

'Elephant Drug. The name's on all the labels now.'

'It rings a bell. I've seen one.'

'You find them in the P. K. Rayner stores, they're part of the chain.'

Knowledge settled down over me like a storm cloud, and my muscles stiffened. Pete Harman was studying me soberly.

'My God, Pete,' I said, 'you're not so crazy are you? I saw Petreen at P. K. Rayner today. She had some kind of bust-up in the business office.'

'I was on the street looking for her car to show on the hospital lot.'

'You were waiting for Petreen.'

'To pay her the cash.'

'No way you're paying Miss Petreen a cent, my friend. Let's go find her.'

We cabbed back to Compton, but Dr Petreen was not available. The receptionist, trying to smile for me while being stern with the patient, admitted the doctor'd called in sick a little earlier. No, her address could not be released for obvious reasons.

The phone book was no good either, and my energy was flagging. I let Harman pay cash at a motel on Hermosa Beach. They had a diner there with acceptable steak and fries. The TV set worked. So did the shower. I soaped a lot of sour sweat down the plughole. We reckoned Elephant Drug would open at 9.30 in the morning. I lay down on the time machine and waited.

17

IT felt strange, waking in an LA motel with Pete Harman. My body had crudely grabbed slumber from my mind and left it unrefreshed. The idea that I was onto a motive for Peppi's snatching had kept me restless.

'I have to call Sal,' I stated from my twin bed.

'Let's get out a here and go someplace down the road,' Harman said.

'We'll go to P. K. Rayner now,' I said.

They'd launched the sun over Phoenix and it was stirring the LA suburbs as the cab drove through. There were garbage pickup trucks, streetcleaning rigs, early commuters on swing shifts, a couple of male joggers with shiny faces and a few bums kicking tin cans and thinking about taking a flop in the park.

Like partners on one-night stands, the commercial streets looked their worst at dawn, grimy linear rubbish tips of unlit neon, tattered hoardings, empty parking spaces and formula-built bank foreclosures.

Ten minutes later we were passing a blacktop desert as wide as a stadium car lot, and staring at a ten-storey stack of chocolate-coloured cubes and gold mirror-glass boxes. It was topped with a rank of flagpoles all hung with droopy Old Glories. In big letters on the facade it said P. K. RAYNER. In little neon letters way below it said The Has Bean. The Has Bean was a coffee shop built at the entrance to the atrium of the department store. Harman tapped the cabbie and pointed.

The place was nearly all tinted glass. A small wetback teenager in a blue nylon coat was sponging the floor and there was a bullet-headed fellow with shoulders like bolsters gearing things up behind the counter.

I went to the phone booth in a niche at the end of the room. It had the usual sour hangover of failure. The phone is a hope machine that can suck away hope as well. The receiver felt clammy to the touch and the mouthpiece disease-ridden against my chin. My credit-card number seemed to belong to a different citizen than me. The tone sounded for an age, then it stopped and Sal's voice said: 'Yeh.'

I opened my mouth to tell him where I was and nothing came. Some things you want to know too much.

'Who's this?' Sal said.

My name came out right. Then the question.

'Sure,' he said. 'She's helping mind the horses at the Christian Riding School up in the Kawailoa Forest. Della saw her there last week. Thought I might go up myself, see 'bout doin' some trail ridin' work at weekends, seeing as how the Pooka's all busted up and they don't seem to have no plans to rebuild the place . . . Hello?'

A pay phone doesn't provide much leverage when your legs go. I came to rest with my shoulder wedged in the corner of the niche.

'Can she come to the phone?'

''Course not, I'm at my place. I reckon she'd be stayin' in the barn t'day, it's bin rainin' blue blazes.'

'Can I call her?'

'You kidding? A roof with no walls, and a harness room is all there is. Horses don't make calls as rule.' His yucking noise echoed fifteen hundred miles across the Pacific. 'Seriously, I don't know where she's shacked up. It's too far to work from the coast.'

'What sort of . . . shape's she in?'

'Hell, Della said she's okay. Seems like the dope farmers gave her a hard time partyin' but she kin take care of herself.'

I swallowed. It tasted sour but I got out a request for Della's telephone number. Sal didn't have it. She was nearly dead, about twenty-eight years old. I told him to call my Santa Flora number

99

if he heard any more news. And I told him if he saw Peppi to tell her my number. She might have lost it.

We said goodbye, the phone clicked over to dial tone in my hand and the bitter smell of thousands of failed communications wafted off it.

I reached my home number and worked the remote controller. No messages came over.

I could have gone and bought a quart of hooch and drunk myself blind. I had scars on my skull, aches in my bones and a pain in my heart. No way did I believe that she and Einstein and his hairy cohorts could have spent any time partying together. Why wasn't she back working at the beach? That body started pawing the ground and whinnying if she didn't swim it at least a mile every day. I hung up.

Harman wasn't around. Bullethead was at the counter setting up a pair of cups and saucers with a tub of half 'n' half and two packets of sugar cubes for each. He inclined his head past the phone niche at a wrought-iron spiral staircase installed to give the place a moody atmosphere. It went up through a six-foot diameter hole in the varnished pine ceiling. I went over and climbed it far enough to poke my head through. Still no sign of Harman at the tables above. I peered down between the steps and Bullethead threw me a cheesed-off look.

'In the john,' he growled. He was adorable. I went back and slid into a bench halfway along the window that looked out on ten acres of hardtop. The view suited the bleak frame of my mind. The gray desert was painted with white grid lines like a battle cemetery. The plots were bare except for one solitary car which was parked halfway to the highway.

Stablehand was nice work, but not as a prisoner. I had two white horses at Santa Flora, and the first thing I planned to do when I got Peppi home was wake her at dawn and take her out on the rear terrace overlooking the back fifty I leased under the slopes of the Santa Lucia range, let off a four-finger ball-game whistle, and bring those gray Anglo-Arabs out of the pine brush a hundred yards away at a lick. Watch them prance over with their manes combing the breeze, heads bucking, nostrils flaring for joy and haul up a-whinnying and frisking hello as we held out pieces of cake-feed for their velvety muzzles to snuffle up.

Five miles away a jumbo sloped up from LA International, the invisible sun behind me flashing off its highlights, and I felt a pang of desire to move, as though if I failed to act soon, I might not move for a long time. A whiff of coffee hit me; Bullethead had brought the two cups to the table and was pouring mine. He left Harman's cup empty.

I took a sip, but it was too hot. They had pills for my condition at Compton, and they'd be coming on sale four or five decks up at Elephant Drug when we went to check it out, but for now I poured my coffee into Harman's cup, blew on it and tipped it back into mine so it was still hot but I got a better hit. Harman's drained cup looked as though he had emptied it and gone. Out in the atrium two uniformed security guards were conferring beside a brown brick basin which supported a forty-foot-high honeycomb made of aluminium tubing and amber-tone plastic, down which water gushed during trading.

The waterfall reminded me of the spiral staircase. I looked over my shoulder at it, and decided to follow it up to the john.

There were two urinal basins with fresh white deodorant rings lying in them, a handbasin with no mirror, a soap dispenser, hand-drier and three-drawer Ramses dispenser offering plain, ribbed and colour-variety packs, and a john with the door closed and a foot pressing up against it wearing a tie-up black leather shoe with no string in it.

The door wouldn't open. I shoved harder and there was a noise of shoes scraping on tiles as it gave wide enough for my shoulder to get in.

His eyes were half closed, his jaw lolled and his head slumped: he could have been very nearly dead of a cold, but he was nearly cold and very dead. His shirt sleeve was pulled high and had been split to bind into a tourniquet. A disposable syringe hung by its needle from a vein in his scarred white forearm, its contents a quarter injected. The other hand lay open as if inviting me to give the plunger a squeeze. A vial filled with clear fluid lay on the tiled floor.

I took care of the vial and the syringe, pulled undone the tie round his waist, hunkered him over my shoulder and worked his pants and underwear down to his knees, opened the lid of the can, set him down on the seat and rested his freckled head against the cistern. It didn't look right so I doubled him up over his knees and let him loll against the wall. Then I swung round, took a deep lungful of toilet smell mingled with death and moved out of the room.

18

'GET a cab for my pal, he's passed out in the john,' I said, laying a $100 bill on the counter. Bullethead stayed put and reached for the phone beside the cash register. At this early hour a cab might not take long, but not long for a cab was long enough for me to get out of sight.

Silently saying goodbye to Peter Harman and feeling the wads of bills in my coat pocket, I headed out across the hardtop desert in the direction of the airport. It seemed original to walk five miles in a town where few people walked fifty feet. There was no chance of being mugged. No mugger could get that lucky.

The solitary car got closer. It was a cream Alfetta Sprint in good condition, which said something to me, but the voice was fuzzy. I kicked the controls of my mind like a duff television set. People dying upset me. I had to stop and peer inside. Dr Petreen was slumped against the driver window.

There was a misty patch on the glass by her cute little nose, and her hands were tucked tidily into the pockets of her black car coat. She was not dead, she was having a little dawn nap in the middle of an attractive parking lot. I felt an urge to make a little mist patch of my own. The urge made me try the handle of the passenger door. It came open. I got into the bucket seat and said: 'Airport, James.'

'What the – ' With tousled hair, angrily flashing cross-eyes, she shone a nightmare at me.

'I could say the same,' I said. 'Those nice men in suits told you not to come back here, remember?'

'I fell asleep, goddammit.' She was telling chiefly herself. After pulling back her black cashmere cuff to check a Cartier gold wristwatch and cursing in an unladylike fashion she twisted the engine into action, bashed the stubby gearshift and threw us forward with whiplash force towards the highway. Twenty yards away a cab was turning in towards the P. K. Rayner department store and The Has Bean. There was no need to tell her to accelerate. When we'd put a couple of miles between us and P. K. Rayner I asked her to turn off into a service lane at the back of a bunch of tacky warehouses. We stopped beside a row of tall steel garbage hoppers.

I let her have it. 'Peter Harman's dead. He snuck into the john back there to shoot up. Whatever they sold him at Compton, less than half an ampoule of it killed him. He never finished the fix.'

She pulled something out of her fashionably raked pocket and showed it to me. It had a muzzle that looked like the tiny asshole of the world, ready to dump.

'Okay, whatever your name is. Where's Penelope Harman?' she said.

I found I'd raised my hands. I put them down again.

'For crying out loud, I'm busting a gut trying to find out where she is and what's going down,' I protested.

'Didn't Pete Harman tell you?' she blazed.

'How the hell could he?'

'How the hell could he?' she mimicked meanly. I was confused, but I didn't whine the way she made out. Her pulling a gun upset me. 'He happens to be her father and he just came into at least ten million,' she snapped.

I shrugged.

Petreen was so disgusted, she put the gun away on me.

I felt I'd failed, and tried to catch up.

'He's dead back there,' I stated, pointing.

'Did you get a look at his pupils?'

'Yeah.'

'How were they?'

'So small they were almost gone.' I saw the dazed surprise in Harman's eyes again. Two blue planets on white china, with tiny specks at the centre.

'Atropine,' she muttered, staring out the windshield at nothing. 'High-strength insulin, maybe.'

'He has a lot of tracks.'

'Yes,' she said. 'They won't bother to call the patrol car.'

'No postmortem?'

'Compton'll pick up the body from the morgue.'

'They do postmortems?'

'Of course. The insane are mostly old. Young patients are high priority for research. Thousands of dollars in drugs go into their brains.'

'Would they report a murder?'

She swivelled her face round to lock onto mine. Her strabismus seemed to cut down across my gaze from two unrelated rivet holes. The nervy, pretty mouth was showing a tiny twitch. Then, as I'd seen her do before, she found my focus in parallax, which released a depth charge through her and along the ether to me. She was lush blackness looking into my soul. Completely nakedly. I got a rush of excitement.

'You wouldn't, would you,' I said.

'No.'

'Because you control the pharmacy.'

She nodded. I rocked with it.

'Because you issue the skag.'

Nodding.

'Because you're a bent shrink.'

'I was.'

'Because you were. What are you now?'

'A trust-buster.'

'What's that mean?'

The look went away. It was like having Aladdin's treasure chest slammed shut in my face. She pushed the gun deep into her pocket, twisted ignition and rammed shift. We burned rubber all the way to the next block, where she turned the way that went away from the airport.

'Hold it, I want the airport.'

'You hold it, whatsyourname.'

Fight ebbed out of me as gravity massaged my body into the form-hugging bucket seat. We ran two reds, rode into the rising sun with the stumps of downtown off to the left, made two rights in a row and came out onto a highway overlooking P. K. Rayner from the rear, where the parking lot was only fifty yards deep and there was a big freight area wired off, next to a set of waste-offload bays with hoppers of garbage and heaps of bulging black bin liners and bundles of flattened boxes.

She parked so that we were in the shadow of a slot machine arcade called Family Leisure Centre, which was wire-screened, empty and unlit. Behind P. K. Rayner two eighteen-wheelers were backed up to the freight bays. Other bays were vacant with their doors hauled shut.

'They may have a make on your car,' I said.

'Watch the freight bays,' she replied.

A blond guy in green coveralls slung himself up into the cab of one of the trailers and swung back out again, shaking something. Up on the deck he shook it again and a business suit who moved out from behind the trailer took a stick out, placed it in his mouth and gave it a light. They were joined by a guy in a brown work coat carrying a clipboard.

'Recognize anybody?'

I checked Petreen's porcelain-doll silhouette and found it expressionless.

'Should I?'

There was a pause. The three men on the loading bay wagged their heads and shifted apart, turning to go their own ways. The driver made for his cab, the business suit walked into the shadows and the clipboard man stood checking a stack of packing cases.

'You said you met Jayne Maronek.'

'That's right, I did.'

Yesterday. Or was it the day before that? My intellect shone like a three-way bulb turned down.

'Did you meet . . . '

Dr Petreen's pause charged the car with energy.

' . . . Mr Maronek?' I said.

I imagined the Maronek woman saying, My Husband's In Security, with the electric door sliding closed past her V-neck.

Petreen was nodding, her whole face pinched.

'Does he work at P. K. Rayner?'

She made a little choking sound, like a corpse trying to laugh, but her eyes stayed on the freight yard.

'Watch the truck.'

The cab was facing us. When it started up and turned towards the highway exit, the trailer was brought sideways on. Big letters there read ELEPHANT DRUG, and underneath it said *A Division of P. K. Rayner.*

'The other one could be a P. K. Rayner truck. The drugstore uses the same yard.'

'Pete Harman was hip to this setup?' I said.

'All the P. K. Rayner stores have their own deliveries except Elephant Drug, which is headquartered here.'

She left a pause and I felt I was failing again. Patrol cars seemed to be lurking behind every building in sight, like a computer game in my brain.

'It means drug products come directly here from bond at Long Beach,' she said. 'So does everything else, from refrigerators to zip fasteners. And it's all inventoried together.'

'I don't get it. So what?'

'That's the beauty of it,' Dr Petreen mused, drilling me with the strabismus like a mad doll.

'Listen,' I said, 'it's clear to me you have at your disposal containerloads of heroin. Now can we go to the airport? I have an appointment with my fiancée to make a baby.' I slipped my fingers under the door latch. She slipped her barrel under my heart.

'Very radical surgery,' she murmured convincingly. I let my hand fall away. She kept the gun where it was. 'If you don't get a grip on what I'm telling you I'll blow your balls off, one by one,' she said.

'It's been a nasty morning.'

'You can rest soon, now listen.' She put the gun away and explained with obsessional intensity, as though she was unloading a dangerous cargo of knowledge. 'If you've got drugs legitimately coming in and out the same door as other goods it's quite easy to filter pharmaceutical supplies elsewhere by reporting shoplifted other inventory, like perfume, records, electronics and so on. All the freight inventory counts is volume. You handle the forms right, you can rake off trailerloads of pharmaceuticals which have been delivered into the country entirely legitimately.'

'So Rayner's another racketeer?' I said. 'Isn't he the big noise on the board of the LA Opera and convenor of a thousand fundraisers?'

'That's the beauty of it,' she said. 'You don't even need to own the store. All you need to control is security, which oversees the inventorying and the so-called theft.'

There was a short silence. We looked at each other. Her skin was bleached and taut, the eyes backlit with fury.

'Maronek's a security man,' I said.

She looked across the street at the freight bays, where the clipboard man had moved to another stack. The business suit came into sight again and pointed out things to the clipboard man, who nodded.

'I was waiting in the parking lot to go in the back and kill him,' Petreen muttered through her teeth. 'Before he flies back north.'

'So that's him,' I said. 'He must make a lot of money on the side, feeding sky to people like you in places like Compton. Why did you kill Pete Harman?'

'I didn't.'

'You were against him. You wanted to lock him up and throw away the key.'

'Maronek was leaning on me about that. I had no reason to spike Pete Harman's fix.'

'What's Maronek got to do with you?'

She kept looking across the road.

'He finds me irresistibly attractive.'

'So you're going to give him the brushoff with that pea-shooter.'

'Placed close to a prefrontal lobe, a liver or a heart, it's effective,' she said with precision.

'What did he do wrong – smile?'

'We had an arrangement.' Looking away. 'He let me down.'

She started to drive. The engine whizzed and charioted us out of the city. I tried to concentrate, but the sky turned a beautiful shade of orange, dissolved, and became a wide Missouri, flowing deep into the heart of things. The world carried on with its noises and bumps and bounces, but nothing untoward rocked my raft on the surface of time.

19

I WOKE a few times before we got to Santa Cruz. Somewhere north of Santa Barbara my body fell onto a heap of flapjacks, eggs, bacon, toast, honey, strong coffee and more strong coffee, and further up 101 it took a leak. I started to come round when we were a couple of headlands from Santa Flora.

'I have to stop and make arrangements for the wedding, Dr Petreen.'

'Okay,' she said, holding the spine of the road at 90 mph like she had for the last five hours.

When we came through Santa Cruz and the sight of the jade-cum-turquoise sea went to my head I started telling her how sorry I was that I wouldn't be able to make her decently welcome at my place, how I'd really like to take her up to see the redwoods in return for her kindly driving me, how much I'd like her to walk the San Mateo beaches and dig California being really two states north and south not one, but how very sorry I was that I had to hurry on over to my bride in Hawaii where she was waiting for me with her tongue hanging out. I rambled on. Maybe she'd popped Quaaludes in my coffee. She played along like she had, saying, 'Sure, sure.'

When we got near Santa Flora, which she could tell because a motel two miles south on the coastroad is called the Santa Flora Hideaway, and there's a trailer place called the Santa Flora Sands a ways further on, she held the wheel with one hand and used the other to stick her automatic up against my heart from behind my arm.

'Sorry, we won't be stopping,' she said.

'I forgot you had the piece,' I complained.

She said: 'If I squeeze . . . you forget you lived.'

'Does it matter?'

The first time I'd ever said or meant the words. Dr Petreen could blow me away when she felt like it and trained on corpses she should make a clean job of it.

The morning traffic was tied up not far from the turn-off to my place, so she had to brake down to 20 mph, then ten, then she wasn't doing much more than walking pace, so I brushed away the gun, opened my door, hauled myself out of that form-fitting bucket seat and started up the bank.

She was as good as her word and shot me, accurately. Hit in the left leg, and only having one other available, I pogo-sticked back down into the storm gutter and fell over on my shoulder.

She left the car running and came hurrying round to drag me back into the passenger seat. It seemed likely she might fire again, so I let her drag. Having got out with two good legs, I got back in a few seconds later with one. It seemed like a waste of effort, and another dismal failure by Wallace. She let in the clutch to catch up with the car ahead.

'Tear your pant leg off, I have to see if the artery's hit.'

'Just like that,' I said, looking over my shoulder out of curiosity. There were two guys in fishing caps in a late-model Japanese four-by-four driving behind, who looked bored, as if they were leaving an all-night card game for a roofing contract. Maybe they thought I'd jumped out to grab a gold bar I'd seen lying by the highway and pulled a ligament. It happens every day. I noticed my pant leg going soggy.

Dr Petreen's face had gone the tint of old newspaper. It was frightening to ride with her in a prison cell down Santa Flora's main street, past the Mercs and Ferraris and Porsches and the high-class boutiques, with a hole in my leg. We stopped at the light opposite the offices of Vincent Larosa, my lawyer, but I made no further move to vacate the Alfa. Like me, Petreen clearly no longer cared if she lived or died, and would gladly look the cops in the eye as she emptied her clip in my direction.

My forefingers had worked their way tremblingly into the hole in the chino cloth where the bullet had exited six inches above my knee. I pulled them apart, tearing my pant leg open. Petreen peered over.

'Nice clean surgical intervention,' she said. 'Muscular trauma will keep you out of the marathon for a while. I'll clean it up in a minute. There's flucloxacillin in the trunk.' She accelerated out of the beachside community in which I was a moderately honoured figure, leaving behind my memories of Laurie, my overdrafts, my collector car and my faith in the Santa Flora Police Department. Adrenalin was making me shiver and I was moving through the zone of fear and amazement into anger.

'You're abducting me against my will, that's a felony. You've shot me, that's a felony. What the hell is eating you, lady? If you've got a grudge against Hedwig Maronek why don't you take it out on him? All I want to do is fly to Hawaii.'

'Where is the turn-off to Redwood City?' she cut in.

'Redwood City?' The kaleidoscope of my confused life shifted with a clunk. 'Wait a minute.'

'I guess any of them will do,' she muttered, and threw the Alfa hard right onto the Tunitas road.

'I thought we were blowing town, not heading for somewhere,' I said.

She wrenched us onto the shoulder of a curve which gave a wide, high view of the Pacific and skidded to a halt. I stared at the horizon, trying to see a thousand miles over it. Pain, fended off for a while by shock, was making a big entrance in my left thigh.

Petreen slammed the hatchback and opened my door, holding a metal box with a red cross printed on it. We had an argument about my pants, in the end I took them down and let her clean the entry and exit wounds, dress them and bandage my leg. She got out a hypodermic syringe and demanded that I let her give me an injection of painkiller. I refused.

'It needs antibiotics, too,' she said.

'Shoot my balls off instead,' I told her. 'I do not trust a Compton needle.'

Pain was bringing some focus into the blurred puzzle of my

life. I lifted my knee gently up and down as we followed the bends up the ridge.

'I get it now,' I said, after a few miles.

'You do?'

'You and Maronek must've had a scene going. He kept your little sideline at Compton supplied with ripped-off pharmaceuticals and you kept him supplied with pussy on the side. Only he was getting into deeper water than he realized with you so he gave you the kiss-off.'

No reaction.

'You threatened to expose him but he gave you a short course in what power was about. You were out of a job overnight and cut off from your tax-free benefits, probably with a bent lawyer tipping off the revenue. So you got out your popgun and went down to perform persuasive terminal surgery on him at his office.'

She picked up a pair of sunglasses from the dash and put them on, not varying her reckless speed.

'That's where Peter Harman comes in. After I told you he was dead, we two suddenly became inseparable. Why?'

She kept looking ahead and said with a hard edge: 'Hey boy, you ever been raped by a woman? 'Cause if I raped you, you'd die.'

I took hold of her sleeve and yanked it up her arm, grabbing her hand off the wheel at the same time and twisting her forearm veins towards me. The tires brayed as she wrestled us back onto the highline with one slender fist.

'Tracks look old to me,' I said. 'So you're an old-time needle freak, huh? How'd you rig your exams? Pussy on the side for the professor?' Dodging her energetic backslap threw me against the door and wrenched my leg. 'So now you think you caught something off a spike and you're lethal. Come on, spit at me!'

She launched an explosion of sputum my way.

I grabbed my leg and taunted her: 'Spit on my wound!'

She expectorated more accurately at my torn pant leg.

I gave her the straight question: 'How *did* you get it?'

'The same way Maronek did,' she snarled.

'Oh, that kind of injection.'

Her knuckles were white on the wheel, the little face contorted by revulsion.

The words were torn out of me: 'God damn it, I feel sorry for you.'

'Shut up with the pity, pimplebrain,' she snapped back. 'It's you that's in trouble, not me.'

20

THERE was no point in quibbling; I had troubles. Peppi hadn't sent a message out with her girlfriend and nor had she called. Somehow she was trapped in a stables way-the-hell-and-gone into the mountains. Einstein and his committee were in the picture, and my wounded leg was stiffening up. Dr Petreen was booting us at full speed towards Cahill Ridge, a homicidal woman in some kind of terminal despair.

My plan of action was as hazy as the cloudbank we drove into as we climbed. I let her climb. After her long spell at the wheel I judged it wiser to bag my head. For a long time I tried to channel the pain in my left thigh into the Alfa's straining engine, hoping it might cause metal fatigue. I took the odds on whether she would repair any breakdown with a bullet in my head, because it seemed I was being delivered somewhere, even if the destination was one I preferred to leave hidden in the haze.

As we turned onto 84 and started snaking downhill the weather cleared to show a Northern California sun chasing ahead over the peaks to our right. Signs blatantly shouted we were on the way to Redwood City. Still I said nothing, letting an idea take shape on its own. None did.

We entered newly gashed hillside townhouse territory and passed through it into sloping villa tracts which in turn gave way to condo country and department stores, with the occasional indication of unrepaired earthquake damage still visible here and there. She confidently crossed the old bungalow underbelly of Redwood City and forked back westwards into slopes of prairie-style villas and split-levels. We entered a maze of crescents and connectors which she picked her way through more unsurely. After a few confused full circles and three-point turns we were heading towards a curving incline which was marked Diadem. She turned the wheel and thumped us against the incline with an impact that loosened many chassis weldings plus a couple of my own.

She passed the gate marked 3296 and swerved into the open drive, hitting the gradient with another frame-busting bang and burning rubber to get us up onto the forecourt of the three-car garage, which contained the scruffy brown Toyota and the oyster 1950s Cadillac that I remembered from an earlier call.

'You don't need to point that at me,' I said.

'Move,' was her answer. The human look was back, no trembling lip and taut sense of fuss, no searing strabismus. Her eyes were dilated passionately, but not the kind of passionately I would have preferred; it was the desire you would see in the eyes of a hungry moray eel. The Alfa's engine clicked with relief as it cooled; I hoped it would detonate.

With the automatic she waved me out.

I stayed put. 'Get me to a hospital, doctor. You're already on your way to jail, but if you act professionally now you might just save your licence for another day.'

'It's a flesh wound, and I've first-aided it, and you refused painkiller. Now stiff-leg it over there.'

She nodded towards a wall of windows under the projecting eaves of the house's low-pitched hip roof. The plate-glass front door slid back on cue, revealing a tough-looking individual wearing tinted spectacles with steel rims. He failed to conceal his powerful frame with a fawn cardigan over a white rollneck, navy slacks and fancy striped-leather Oxfords. The top of his hard loaf looked as if it had been blown off and replated: it was a plateau grassed with thin maidenhair, with tufty regular-type hair thrusting up on either side. There was a vertical fold down the top of his face which seemed to reach out fifteen paces and grab me by the throat. As he moved forward I recognized the gait: it was Hedwig Rupert Maronek.

He approached in a hurry, hauled the driverside door open

and peered into the muzzle of Dr Petreen's cute little lady's model, the one which had worked so effectively on my thigh muscles. Maronek's eyes, black buttons behind the spectacles, shifted past the weapon and fell on the fresh work it had done. He was held for a moment as the tension inside the Alfa clutched him in an acrid, electrical rush, then he stepped back from Dr Petreen, pointing at her and shaking his head.

'Don't do anything crazy, bitch,' he muttered respectfully.

She brushed off her face the black bang that must have driven her cross-eyed over the years, passed the gun into her right hand and placed the muzzle against my temple. I bridled, but she kept pointing.

'Take a good look at him,' she said. 'He's Peppi's loverboy. Going to take us where the little girl's hiding.'

She said nothing more, but abruptly leaned over and smacked her forehead onto my wound. My yawp echoed down the car frame and my back arched like a rutting nymphomaniac's.

Maronek reached a beefy hand in to seize her by the scruff of the neck where he had rabbit-punched her, and hauled her bodily out of the car like a puppet, relieving her of the gun, which he pocketed. With a bunch of collar in one hand and a twist of skirt and panty round the gluteal fold in the other he hustled her staggering and crumpling into the house.

There was no weapon in the glove compartment and I'd already checked surreptitiously round the floor. Her Italian black leather shoulder bag was on the rear jump seat but pain stabbed me back from turning to reach it.

The medical kit in the trunk contained the pair of daggerlike scissors she had used on my dressings. My right leg stepped out and I threw my weight after it, dragging the other leg behind me like a red-hot ball and chain. Clawing my way along the car's guttering, I made it to the hatchback and pushed the button. There was a clunk and I manipulated the lid open, supporting half my weight on the rim.

The case was light enough, but it was difficult to get it out with a hatchback being slammed down on my hands.

Clasping the more seriously bruised of my wrists, I rotated 180 degrees on my good leg and flopped like a beached seal onto the paving where Maronek drop-kicked my bellybutton against my spine.

He picked my head up by the short hairs and twisted my face towards his. 'You wait here, okay?'

He came right back with a one-wheeled yard buggy and used some effort to hoist me into it, shoulders first, then by the knees, so that I was sprawled on my back, and he trundled me into the house. The first thing I saw through a red gauze of pain when he tipped me out was one of Mrs Maronek's cigaret butts trodden into the buff shag carpet six inches from my nose, its Tampax-like filter tip dipped in blood-coloured lipstick. Beside it was a small foot in black nylon, wearing a gray fashion shoe that had come unstuck from its high heel.

'That's real smart,' its owner said. 'Damage the goods so they don't operate. That's all you know how to do, is declare goods damaged. Now one of my cerebral vertebrae is dislocated.'

'I never declared you damaged.'

'Not on purpose. I need a lab test, and I think you should pay, I think you should pay a pile.'

'Oh shit, you want Compton back that bad?'

'You made me damaged goods, you scum, what else've I got?'

'Less than you think. Since you dropped round yesterday there's been an accident in the systems room and the evidence is down the tube. P. K. Rayner's inventory records have been corrupted.'

'You corrupt everything.'

'Don't be naive.'

'I'm getting smarter, I brought this guy along.'

'Damaged, though.'

'Yeh, I catch on real quick, huh?'

'Shame is he's no good to me while Peter Harman's runnin' looser'n a hound dog round the streets of LA just because you can't get it together to put him in a soundproof cage and throw away the key.'

'That's not a problem any more, Heddie.'

There was a pause and I looked up. Maronek chortled, punched his hand and ground the fist in like he was making squashed-fly soup.

'Bad habits caught up with him, huh? They pulled it off.'

He paced up and down, then stopped. Having them both stare at me was like lying in a grave with the mourners peering down.

'I better get this guy shaped up.'

Maronek's Bally casuals came near my head and his beefy hands groped under my shoulders. He got my back across his knee and heaved me back towards the davenport.

I wrapped my arms round his knees in a backward tackle and twisted hard, using the good leg for leverage. The cut-glass ashtray on the Maronek woman's coffee table felt even heavier than it had looked as I swiped it off, propelling myself forward to bring the corner of it down along with a shower of ash and butts onto Maronek's cranium.

It was my wrist which was weak, not the glass heavy. The ashtray bounced off Maronek's skull as he butted the bridge of my nose. We collided, but I sailed on through him into darkness.

When I came to I was up against the davenport and they were scrapping some more, but physically, with her clawing at him as he wrenched the jacket off my shoulder and yanked my arm out of its sleeve. She was hissing and squinting into his ear, like a warped voice of conscience.

'I can't allow it, I can't allow it, I can't allow it.'

The free hand, marked with a disc of fresh Band Aid six inches up the forearm, shoved my shirt sleeve up to near the shoulder. The other steadied a syringe loaded with dark crimson fluid, a glob of which hung on the point. Something screamed, short and sharp. It was me.

'Blow my brains out,' I bellowed, clamping a fist onto his needle wrist. 'Not that!' I had a flash of Hans's Fijian begging his father to strangle him. 'Don't bury me alive with the fucking plague!' I bawled to the whole world, willing it to hear.

He was on his knees frowning, mouth agape, engrossed in the task of rubbing his thumb against a point below my armpit, trying to shrug off my impeding grasp with his needle elbow, which squirted a tiny lick of red snake tongue from its prong.

'What the hell's this, Hedwig?'

His mate's voice rapping up from the basement staircase threw Maronek for a second, long enough for Petreen to tip him away from me. The Maronek woman crossed the room, leaned down and put a large, high-tech automatic against her man's temple, displaying the gaping cleavage under the same V-neck sweater I'd seen before. It looked a shade dirtier. She held the weapon with calm assurance as she faced the upside-down lenses at me and Petreen and back at Maronek who, having a weakness for dangerous women, was keeping still.

'What plague?' she snapped at him.

'The same one he gave me,' Petreen snarled, twisting the syringe away from him.

Jayne Maronek poked her barrel up under the steel frames into her husband's eye socket and peered into his pupils across it. He radiated hatred back.

Adrenalin worked my bad leg like a jet-powered prosthetic device. I was up and across the shag like a cheetah before she fired with a deadened digga-digga-digga report that thwacked three slugs in microsuccession into the wall over the open plate-glass door as I went through it.

'Don't shoot!' Petreen and Maronek were shouting.

I left them to explain to Jayne Maronek why she shouldn't be shooting, reckoning the Alfa's fuel gauge showed just enough dregs to get me to San Francisco International at speed.

21

THE taxi stand in the shadow of the ramps at Honolulu International was nose to tail and so was the queue of waiting passengers. I limped twenty yards eastwards to the limousines commissionaire, a big fellow whose uniform and expression would have gone down okay in the Lubianka jail in preglasnost Moscow. He accepted with professional unconcern the $500 I handed him, and muttered instructions into his walkie-talkie. A stretch Lincoln in deep blue came onstream and pulled alongside like a cool piece of night-time being drawn across the day. I poked an extra hundred into the uniform coat breast pocket and got a salute as I ducked into the interior gloom.

The driver looked round and we locked eyes. It was the wayward stare of an old hobo looming out of a gaunt-boned, twenty-seven-year-old face. Chunks of ill-cut blond hair stuck down over a stalk of neck from the chauffeur cap. 'Man,' Sal said.

I counted off ten bills and handed them over, kneeling on the floor. 'Make Waimea Bay.'

He gunned it. Somehow I got over into the front seat.

When we were past Pearl Harbor and up on H2 heading north, I said: 'This the new gig?'

'Done it before,' he told me, and looked down at my leg, where there was a blood stain the size of a quarter-dollar spreading on the chinos I'd bought at San Francisco airport. 'How much trouble we lookin' at, man?'

I picked up the carphone and keyed in a number I knew by heart.

Hans replied in his dignified way, like Erich Von Stroheim playing the butler: 'Regner speaking.'

'Hans, it's me, I got past the cops at the airport. I've come back to get Peppi Harman.'

There was a pause before Hans replied. He sounded detached, like a satellite connection in time-lapse.

'Cody, my boy . . . It's good to hear you . . . I had to let your room . . . I need the rent you know . . . '

He seemed to be reassuring himself about a remote personage called me.

'Hans, forget the room, where's Ilsa?'

'With me,' he said doubtfully, and added: 'She had to go out a few minutes ago.'

I told him I'd be right over, and pressed cancel on the phone.

Sal used the 55-lane at 110.

'Where you bin?' he asked.

'Doing the family rounds in California,' I said, watching three propeller-powered military freighters circling the Waianae range on their inscrutable exercise gyres. 'Peppi got snatched, I'm still not sure who by.'

'But like I told you, Della saw her a few days back.'

'Did she say much?'

'No.'

'Does that sound right?'

'I don' know.'

'Can she live without sea?'

'I guess not.'

'So what the hell's with the horse work just like that?'

'Well, those actor guys . . . '

'What actor guys?'

'That took her away . . . '

'She knew those freaks?'

'I heard they did a kinduva radical show on Ford Island, got theyselves throwed off the base by the navy MPs.'

I pictured Einstein and his men. Had I been part of the show? The future looked like a wall, with Peppi behind it.

We glided into Mokuleia Beach Road and stopped under my old rooms, outside the garage door.

'Turn this mother round somehow,' I said, and limped along the garden perimeter, using the cotton and breadfruit plants to sneak into the lee of Regner's house, where I stood paying full attention.

Sal's limousine purred and its tyres burst gravel like popcorn as it made the multipoint turn. The top fronds of the coconut palms stirred lazily in the afternoon sea breeze and offshore the surf made restful breathing sounds. My left thigh throbbed as loudly as any of them as I moved forward to the verandah.

A sharp snap, the storm door closing, froze me against the shiplap wall – there were footfalls overhead, followed by silence. The shadows showed a figure leaning on the parapet, looking out to sea. When it stood erect, clearly outlined on the lawn, I hobbled forward and said: 'Hans.'

As I mounted the steps he greeted me so feebly I closed in like a magnet to grasp the wide shoulders.

'Need a Swiss action,' he muttered. 'They diagnosed me for a pacemaker, yesterday, at University Hospital.' The effort of telling me made him wheeze for oxygen. His head could have been carved in gray stone. He was a brittle relic of himself, ready to fall to pieces on impact.

'What happened?' I steered him to a cane chair and sat him down.

'We went to Kauai, Ilsa wanted to work – at least, that's what she said. She was in some kind of trouble, though.' He looked up at me and the trouble showed in white lines of blindness marring his irises.

I said: 'She seemed kinda buddy-buddy with Lieutenant Lau about seeing me off the island.'

Hans winced and blanched a shade grayer, making me regret my harshness.

'She's not been herself for a while,' he muttered, using his right hand to stroke his left arm. 'I regretted very much what happened, and so did she, but . . . ' he tried to crank some dignity into his shrunken frame ' . . . you took the law into your own hands, barging in here, using my gun for a crazy piece of mischief – '

'Hold it, Hans,' I warned. 'That's Ilsa's line you're dishing up. How about getting my angle?'

He sat rubbing in sullen assent.

'Burglars were trampling all over this house anyway,' I said. 'It was academic whether I took the gun or not – and I certainly did not take it for any piece of half-baked kamikaze spy work. I went after Peppi, but somebody set me up to get me off the island and out of their hair. I'd like to know what it has to do with Ilsa. Where is she? What kind of trouble's she in?'

Hans Regner took a deep breath. 'She'll never confide in me about her worries.' He frowned. 'One thing, she thinks she knows who was rifling this place.'

'Who?'

'Well, she won't say. She's been very tense, very stressed, since then. Because of it I had the heart attack.'

'You did have one.'

'Yes.' He mustered a weak grin. 'I've lost count of them, and you don't get any younger.'

'The burglaries, the tension – '

'Inspector Lau came.'

'To Kauai?'

The dazed old man in front of me nodded to save words.

'There was a scene. I was out on the beach. When I got back, Lau had left Ilsa in a very upset condition. I tried to calm her down. Then I collapsed and it was her turn to look after me.' He shook his head and complained: 'A girl like her should never have married an old man.'

'Maybe she should never have left East Germany,' I said, and the anxious note jarred. He packed some of his fear in a glance and threw it back.

'She's not from there originally, either,' he muttered.

'I thought she was from Berlin.'

'She was. I met her there, and she was working there for several years. But she's actually a Russian. What they call an ethnic German.'

'Where's she gone now?' I asked him.

He shoved some time over his shoulders with his hands. 'She took off in the car a while ago, not in the usual way, not for bridge or shopping or visiting. She hurried away, leaving me.

She raced the engine, kicked up gravel.' He sat looking as though she had driven over his body in the street.

'Did Lau give you the Webley back?'

He snorted weakly. 'No.'

'I need something.'

'Where are you going?'

'I think I may be going after Ilsa.'

Briefly he set about gathering the force to resist me, and gave up the struggle. He muttered in a defeated way: 'There's a Japanese officer's automatic in the cabinet, it takes ·32 slugs, you'll find a case of them in the desk drawer.'

I fetched it, with a case of shells. It was all black, with a metal haft. The clip had an unusual catch, full of Nipponese craft.

'It has to be fifty years old,' I said uncertainly, hefting it.

'Hand-turned, good as the day it was made,' Hans growled, waving me away.

Sal waved me away, too.

'Hey, man, no gunplay, we want love, peace, Perry Stroyka, right?'

'Boot it.'

I had the window open, inhaling raspberry-flavour day and ogling playschool clouds. After the visit with Hans, life felt sweet. Even heading after Einstein it felt sweet. Heads turned in Haleiwa, but no sheriff's men. We cruised past the beach.

'Hey, the Pooka's gone.'

'They bulldozed it, man. Yesterday.'

Waimea slipped past, and in a couple of minutes I was climbing towards the Koolau range again.

22

'MAN, what *is* that thing?'

'Depends.'

'What you mean, depends?'

'Depends what you mean when you say what it is.'

'Uh-huh . . . Looks sump'n like a space launch from underground, freeze-frame, like.'

'You got it.'

'I got it?'

'I think so. I thought it was an observatory. Now I figure it's part of the space program. The one like a rocket's communications, but sealed in, see, so you can't read anything from the discs and aerials and suchlike, the way you could if they were out for everybody to look at. And the other one, the penis, is tracking gear, computers, signals, encodement, printers, faxes – no damage to the gates from being rammed by a car, I notice.'

'Yeah?'

'All part of our famous Strategic Defense Initiative, which is part of military espionage, which is the jackboot end of the goose that lays the golden egg.'

'That right? Nothin' t'do with the Peace Corps, huh?'

'No, not the Peace Corps, but there's a Scout Camp supposed to be up this trail. It was me blew the lock off the gate.'

'Why that's right, Nunuloo Camp – hell, they'll have Girl Guides there.'

'Take on two or three in back.'

'Drinks cabinet . . . '

'Rubbers.'

'Cross-ribbed. I drop you here or keep on up this trail?'

'Right on up it.'

'Kinduva long wheelbase for the sticks.'

'You'd never tell we were doing sixty.'

'But maybe the bends, like up there at the head of the valley, it's gettin' curvaceous up thataway.'

'You'll be fine, Sal.'

'This rig's worth a hunnerd fifty thousand. Just the modified windows is fifteen thou – tinted, bullet-resistant.'

'How resistant?'

'I don' know how resistant . . . Resistant, that's all.'

'So how far is the Christian Riding Stables?'

'A ways further in. Not a helluva long way from Waimea Falls. Maybe five miles. Hold it. You intend for me to chauffeur you into those stables?'

'Come on, Sal, we're already halfway there, what's a lick o' dust?'

'Them peaks don't make for good radio.'

'Turn it off.'

'Turn it off?'

'You turn it off all the time, Sal. How about this. Here, I'll put it in the glove box, your boss will be pleased with you.'

'Man, you're flashin' some C-bills. They stiff or f'real? . . . Anyway, how come you hightailed it to the mainland the way you done?'

'I'm no coke trader, Sal, there's no need to look so leery.'

'You wouldn't deal. You too smart fer it.'

'What would I do?'

'You? You'd hustle Hong Kongers out- a that rat-trap they caught in.'

'Hustle Hong – you crazy?'

'Why not? You're the kind, I reck'n. Property. Monkey money. Construction. Tall fucker. You ever ask the Tongs for a job, they'd take you on.'

'Sal, I'm not a heavy. I'm big, but I'm kind of an angel.'

'Swing both ways, huh?'

'Fuck off.'

'You fuck off, man. No, I mean it. Like, are you serious, packing a shooter into the Christian Riding Stables in a limousine – *my* limousine – 'cos you think Peppi Harman's been kidnapped?'

'Listen to me, Sal. I had a feeling about this thing when it happened but nothing like the feeling I get when I wake up in hospital in Honolulu three days later and one Lieutenant Lau of Honolulu PD informs me that I am suspected of espionage but all charges will be dropped if I just leave quietly on the next plane. Which I do. Bandage round brain.'

'Bust your car up?'

'Bust it? Man, I was rammed head-on at 40 mph by a '52 short-box Ford with the gas pedal lashed down, just round about . . . yeah, just round about where we are now. No sign of it, though.'

'They must have come down from the stables. I don't get it, you had a head-on and the fuzz told you it was espionage?'

'Lau said I rammed the space station. It was a blatant con, but what'd he care? I thought he had to be fronting for the pot farmers, but I couldn't figure it out.'

'I can. A big fat rake-off.'

'Sure, but Peppi didn't make sense.'

'Nor does Belkin Spray.'

'Who?'

'The guy who hammered you. The one with the '52 pickup that came and got Peppi. He's Belkin Spray, I remembered his name just now.'

'Why doesn't he make sense?'

'I told you, man, he's a friggin' actor, not a dope farmer.'

'That's what they all say.'

'No way, man, look I know this part of the coast, right? And I tell you this guy Belkin Spray blew in a few months ago. He and his pals were in the news there for a spell, what with the shows they did round Honolulu.'

'What kind of shows, Sal?'

'Faggot shows. Whut d'you expe't?'

'Not faggot shows.'

'Sure, get a bunch of actors, all guys, put 'em in a room, they'll come up with a faggot show.'

'Hey, are we talking about the same guys? The people I dealt with weren't fairies.'

'Lookit you, man, you're no pixie and you're a friggin' *angel*.'

'You reckon – butch punks . . . '

'Gettin' there.'

'Christ . . . '

'The likes o' them turned over half o' San Francisco a few years back. Aydolf Hitler, too, he had 'em in brown shirts runnin' amuck.'

'Slapping me around was like a warm-up.'

'Leather freaks into S/M.'

'Humiliate a straight.'

'Good clean fun.'

'And Peppi.'

'I think one time she said she knew Spray.'

'Why didn't you tell me this before?'

'Shit, man, for me the likes of Belkin Spray can go fuck a duck. I can't see makin' a Bible meetin' outa cornholing. If she said she knew them, it was part of her scene 'bout bein' a dramatic genius. I felt sorry for her for about a millisecond and forgot about it.'

'She said she knew them? When? When you were hearing about the show?'

'Yeah, I reckon.'

'It was kind of a dirty show?'

'Yeah, a gay show. Flute concerto. Gonzel bonanza. Yodelling convention.'

'No females.'

'Sure! Lot o' women who worship fags, go down, dig the show, no sweat. Mostly guys, but a few females o' that sort. Hey, the stables is up here.'

'Sal, keep telling me about Peppi and this guy Spray, I need to get a grip on the scene up there. Spray and his gang are working there, right?'

'I'm guessing. I think they camp out back. Maybe they work. They weren't around when Della was there, 'cos Peppi was talkin' 'bout them. Could be they was off on a trail ride.'

'And she definitely said the guys had taken her along for some heavy partying, nothing else?'

'Seems possible to me.'

'Impossible to me.'

'I see why you wanna take a look. But I don' think you'll find anything outaline. Peppi's cool.'

'Yeh, she is. That's why I'm here.'

'Okay!'

'. . . Sal, did you see that?'

'I saw sumthin', not sure what.'

'A little kid on a go-bike, turning off into the woods?'

'Yeah, that's what it was. Where'd he go? Over the top there? Reckon he's with the stables? There's another! Shite, those li'l bitsy bikes move.'

'I've seen those boys before, they belong to Belkin Spray.'

'Why that's nice. His little chickens'll run back to the coop. He'll know we're coming then, won't he.'

23

THE stables where Peppi had been seen by her friend Della came into view. A hump had taken us over onto a plateau at the end of the valley, surrounded by forested mountain slopes, with the peaks of the Koolau range rearing up bruise-purple behind. The military transporters which spent so long orbiting the range were absent from the sky. Instead there were vultures making ominous parabolas over the head of the valley.

Sal stopped the limousine. The trail led away through ragged woodlands of cork and eucalyptus to a clearing where there was a T-shaped barn of rough-cut timber. One end was partially walled to about eight feet and there was what looked like a storage room walled up to the eaves.

'Are there any glasses?'

'Highball or beer?'

'Field glasses.'

'We have quadraphonic stereo, first-aid kit with morphine ampoules, flashlight, foot pump, you name it.'

'Okay, forget it. You see anyone?'

'Nope.'

'They have hunting rifles, probably a lot else besides.'

'Man, why you talkin' about shootin'?'

'Sal, the shooting's already started.'

His eyes seemed even lighter blue than usual.

'Is that Belkin Spray's bread you're holding?'

'No, it's not. It's Peppi's. I'm here to deliver it.'

131

'Why they want to stop you?'

'Maybe they don't. But I don't see bunting strung up or a hog roasting on a spit, do you?'

Sal turned the ignition key. A slight increase in silence indicated the engine had cut out. I settled a little with the suspension since Sal seemed to be buying in. My blood still bothered him.

'Is that Belkin Spray's hole in your leg?'

'No, that's my hole in my leg.'

'Who put it there?'

'A shrink by the name of Petreen.'

'Why?'

'She objected to me getting out of her car.'

'She?'

'Yeah, she. Sal, I want to skirt around a bit before we go in there. Can you take your side? Go through the trees, get up on the slope so you've got a view, scout round and in from that way? Here, take the gun.'

Keeping his eyes on me, Sal poked two fingers into his jeans pocket and scooped out a hexagonal brass pillbox. With the other hand he fished a gold neckchain out of his T-shirt collar. On the end of it was a miniature ladle. He flipped the box open and conveyed a batch of heaped white powder to each nostril, sniffing sharply each time and rattling his head.

'I don't need your gun,' he said, reaching under the steering column and coming up with a flat black automatic which he unclipped and clipped click-clack like a Mississippi gambler zipping a deck. The long upper ivories appeared and gleamed.

'Tool of the trade,' he said.

'A peacenik know how to use that?'

'Nope.' He winked and opened the door. 'They have walkie-talkies in the trunk, you wanna use them?'

'No. We'll holler.'

'Organic. I like it.'

He slipped away and disappeared into rhododendron brush.

My side of the valley was a hundred yards away. It looked like a mile. After five minutes it felt like it. A candlenut tree leaned against me so I could take pressure off the lead weight which hung from my left hip. Something warbled off to my left making me wish I knew more about bird song. Then I thought of looking out over the treetops. Nothing was flying up, disturbed by movement below. I thanked the tree and moved on.

The slope was worse, and there was undergrowth that hooked tendrils like steel wires round my shins. One of them brought me down, impacting my left thigh against a rock. I plugged my mouth with a fist and backed the scream down into my stomach, where it echoed through my ganglia.

When the red pain-haze cleared and vision returned, I checked the view. The Wallace strategy of gaining height meant I had a great view of bushy treetops and an area of rusty corrugated tin roof. Two vivid red i'iwi birds rose squawking from the slope opposite, indicating that Sal was a hundred yards further along. He had two legs, I had one and a bandaged log.

There was a trail a little further uphill and I used it, because I'd make less noise than plunging around like a rhinoceros in the ivy. Anyway, I didn't want to keep Sal waiting. Abreast of the clearing, I turned downhill through more undergrowth. When I came out of it another candlenut tree leaned against me. I supported it, surprised at how much a limb resented the vectoring of a little piece of lead. I tried to recall the Bible quotation about God knowing every hair on your head. He certainly knew every muscle fiber and nerve ending in my thigh. I was getting acquainted too.

But pride is strong dope and when I made the clearing in the lee of the stables, with Sal thirty yards off standing looking around, holding his gun down by his leg, I stepped out like Gary Cooper in *High Noon*.

'Man, you're gimped,' he said unadmiringly as I approached.

But the way I looked past him, he forgot my lameness, turning to eyeball the gray Volkswagen which was parked behind, halfway into the shelter.

In the shade beyond it, a dozen horses secured by rope halters swished tails and flicked ears at noon flies. But mostly the flies were round the Beetle. The driverside window was wound down and they were riding a regular Oakland Bridge in and out. It gave off a faint freeway hum as I got near. A couple of raiders veered off and made passes at my leg wound. They didn't bother me.

Ilsa Regner did.

She was curled on her side across the driver seat in a sensible Ilsa cotton frock with a gray gingham pattern, her head and arms reaching down into the passenger footwell as if in search of the fuse box.

The fly freeway led to her ear and eyes and nose. Her face was black with them.

We straightened up.

'Coulda bin a heart attack,' Sal whispered. 'Whoever she was.'

It made me wonder who Ilsa was, too.

'I don't think so. I think she came up here looking for what Belkin Spray's got to hide.' I was whispering as well. Sudden death does that.

Sal looked across the clearing, scanning the blind trees. His gaze reached the storehouse and he glanced back at me.

The storehouse door was latched. It had no window. Wordlessly, we both moved ten paces to get to one side of it.

'Hell with this,' he muttered abruptly, and walked along, using his free hand to lift the latch and a foot to kick the door open. He went in. Going out of sight was a betrayal. With my adrenalin level where it was, I walked after him on air.

In the murk there were sacks of feed, with reins, bridles, saddles and other tack hung on the walls. A couple of ledger books lay open on a shelf under a pencil dangling on a piece of string. Shoes stuck out from a pile of sacks by my feet. I nudged them with a toe. They fell over, empty.

The world outside was framed brightly. The billowing slope of mesquite, candlenut and monkeypot forest climaxed in a sky of perfect planetary blue, too perfect. We stepped unreally back into this tourist posterland. The Volkswagen was still there, with the traffic humming through its window. One of the horses whickered and stamped.

Sal was looking at me. He pincered out the pillbox from his pocket, opened it and fished out his spoon all in one movement, offering a little heap of powder. Needing the medicine, I blocked a nostril and sniffed hard. He quickly served himself. Some of the great pressure of disgust in my chest eased. Fear's throbbing swelled, then faded. Thinking became a little easier. Walking, too. Convinced now that the murderers had run, we walked the trail back to the black limousine, which waited sleek and shady, like a hearse.

Inside, with the engine running for the air conditioning, Sal said: 'It's time for the law,' and reached for the telephone.

I gripped his bony wrist.

'Okay. But don't call Sheriff Quilley. Or Lieutenant Lau. I want Ilsa's body taken care of, but keep it anonymous. Just a tip-off, that's all.' I caught sight of the vultures, which seemed to be making their gyres a little closer.

'You know her?'

'Dr Regner's wife. Botanist. Lived on the beach. You've seen her around.'

Salt grunted, shook his head, unhooked the phone, poked a bleep out of it.

'You want me to idennify her?'

I opened the door and got out again.

'No.' I let the door shut while he made the call.

The hills were very quiet. V-for-vulture shadows passed silently over the forest. I listened out carefully for Belkin Spray. I didn't dare listen for Peppi.

24

THE message I got from the silence was to drive further into the mountains.

Sal protested: 'It's forest reserve, nobody lives up there!'

I took out Pete Harman's wad, pulled a few more bills from under the elastic and laid them with the others in the glove compartment.

He didn't stop me, but he still said: 'This vee-hicle has a ten-foot wheelbase.'

'Bullet-resistant windows,' I said, shutting the trap and patting the dash like a dog.

'Shit, man, how'm I gonna explain to dispatch if this hunnerd-fifty-thousand-dollar transportation gets bogged down halfway across a mountain?'

'We'll stick to the trail.'

'And what about coming back, or are you too fired up to think about that?'

'Easy, Sal, we drive in the other direction.'

'Oh yeah? And how do I turn this mother round. Ey? Yo!'

'You reverse out.'

Sal clipped the automatic back under the steering column. I wasn't sure what it meant.

He gripped the steering wheel and wrinkled his nose, huffing out a deep breath.

He put his palms to his cheekbones and dragged the fingers down hard.

He clasped his jean-crotch and worked it. The other hand went under his Hawaiian-shirt armpit and scraped.

He cleared his throat and sniffed, wiping his nose with the back of his arm as if he was fending himself off.

'There's a road atlas under the dash,' he said, and pushed the auto lever forward.

We eased towards the stables, where Ilsa lay dead. Only when Sal had come round and we were moving forward in the cool interior of the limousine could I allow Hans Regner's frail image into my mind. Ilsa belonged to Hans. Ilsa *ran* Hans. Losing her would cut him adrift on an ice floe of old age. It was a double murder. I wondered where the dedicated spy-hunting cop Lau was.

The map showed that the peak ahead of us was Puu Kapu. We were about to cross a dotted line into the Kawailoa Forest Reserve. No highways or trails were marked on the Forest Reserve: users of the atlas were not expected to be hauling logs. A few miles ahead the Kawailoa Reserve turned into the Ewa Forest Reserve. Beyond that the mountains turned into the Schofield Barracks Military Reservation (East Range). I wondered absently what US marines on exercises would make of a black Mercedes stretch limo appearing out of the woods. According to the map the territory held no human habitation whatsoever. There was no route over the mountains to Highway 83 on the east coast. The only way out was north, to our left, past Waimea Falls. That led to the coast. Belkin Spray only raided the coast, he didn't live on it. His move would be to retreat into wilderness, probably onto a dope plantation concealed in the woods for helicopter cover.

We left behind Ilsa's gray Beetle, already part of history, a forensic site framed out there in the warm. The Waimea road wove away to the left, the same kind of hard dirt trail we had come in on. Ahead was a narrower trail, two wheelruts with a rocky crown. Before we'd gone a hundred yards through the forest we'd hit a pothole deep enough to throw both of us against the roof. Sal ground his teeth and drove on.

He had the auto shift in low, and moved at about 30 mph. That way we climbed the slope at the end of the valley, crested a saddleback and tipped down onto the side of another valley and found ourselves surveying primeval Polynesia, only twenty miles from Honolulu. Wide-winged raptors circled over the shoulders of the mountains ahead. Galleonlike balls of cumulus cloud sailed across an enormous Pacific sky under a high sun. As I stared out, an involuntary shiver reminded me that the snort I'd taken in shock at the stables was wearing off, along with the insight I'd enjoyed into the mind of the enemy. Back in the earthly brain of Cody Wallace, I felt a huge weariness. I was in the hotel room in Lahaina, lying down. Peppi was leaning towards me in her white towel robe. The robe was open, revealing her breasts in fragrant shadow. The ocean plunged and withdrew like sex.

'Fuck!'

Sal wound the wheel furiously, but we swooped, banged and veered into the undergrowth, the rear suspension waving and careening after us. Foliage slapped and scraped like bursts of applause. The lanky framework twisted. My weary head hit the roof again and I landed left leg first. My spine took orders from elsewhere and rammed my cranium against the windshield. Somewhere way outside, like a soundtrack, there was a crazed scraping. Things rained against the rear flooring.

'Christ, shit! Holy fuck!'

The car frame barged like a winger with its Ruhr-steel shoulder. Where it had been lurching left, it met something like solid rock and bounced back. The whole vehicle disobeyed the rules of mechanical tranquillity and rebounded, as if it had changed its mind. We slalomed through a blur of tree trunks and undergrowth. From behind its blankets of thick asbestos padding and sheet metal, the V-8 mill bellowed resistance. Our spinning rear wheels made harsh hawking noises like a rubby fighting emphysema in a public toilet.

After we'd weaved along the verge maybe fifty yards, Sal got control of the wheel and wrenched us back on the track. We stopped and waited for something metallic to fall off.

'Goddamn asshole!'

Clutching the wheel still, all his muscles clenched, Sal gazed wildly round the cockpit like Barabbas on the cross.

I let go of my leg and groped around the footwell where the Japanese automatic had been thrown.

He opened up and stepped onto solid ground, looking back.
I got out too, more slowly.

'Some kinda drainage ditch,' he muttered with contempt. He
looked along the flank of the limousine and closed his eyes.

'Oh, fuck.'

'Insurance, Sal,' I drawled. 'Employment for Americans.'

For the first time out he looked at me with goaded anger.

'This is fucking nuts. I need a body shop. You need a doctor.'

He swung into his seat and hauled the door shut. I did the
same, flexing my masseter muscles.

'You can't turn round,' I heard myself saying.

'I fucking well can and I'm fucking well going to, there's
godda be a runoff down this hill for the logging rigs, I can use
that.'

A tremor seized my leg and shook my body with it. The gun
wavered in my grasp. I looked down. The snout wanted to point
at Sal. The forefinger – my forefinger – twisting against the
trigger had no notion of who he was, apart from the two-legged
operator of a four-wheeled vehicle which was headed into Peppi-
land. That sun up there was shining down on her. She had
passed these nameless trees. Somewhere was her living presence;
her voice might be within range even now. I wondered if seeing
Ilsa's corpse had snapped my patience. Still, I laid my left hand
over the barrel and pressed it down on my good leg. We bounced
like that down a thirty-degree incline to the white sound of an
air conditioner on full.

When we levelled out Sal stopped again and got out. I
did likewise, using my right leg. The outside air was clammy,
indecent, urging invaders to strip naked.

'No fucking runoff,' he muttered, glancing wildly back up the
hill.

Ahead, the trail cut through forest in the valley basin and
snaked up the hills the other side.

Aieee-a-a-agh!

For a second – less than that – I thought it was a Hawaiian
bird I didn't know, then right after I knew it for a man, speaking
a universal dialect torn from the gut past human vocal chords –
a pitchless squeal and rattle that locked our eyes across a gulf of
lacquered black steel hood.

'What the – '

Sal broke off and snapped his head up towards the summit of the valley, where a tall forested foothill reared dark green against the purplish peaks beyond.

Huk – Aaaargh! it came again, faint, but searing, drawn from a dictionary all animals are programmed with at birth by a million years of pain.

'It's a man,' I blurted, grasping at a straw of hope.

'Could be,' Sal murmured. 'Could be a sister, too.'

The air tasted poisoned. Even the daylight looked violated.

We got back into the car as one and Sal forced splintered rocks against the undertrunk with every cubic inch he had. The rear view window became engulfed in dust. Ahead, the trail swung left and climbed. At the shoulder of a slope we cut the engine, got out, stood by the roasting hood and tuned in acutely, angling our heads about like aerials.

Nothing came.

We covered about a mile to where the trail crested another saddleback and gave a view of another empty vale. There was a droning like the thrum of marine engines when they are carried far across water to profane a beach. Sal pointed. Two prop-engined military transporters were circling their sacred ground above the crown of the range. One slowly passed below the craggy purple outline, slowly followed by another. Turbo-prop insistence lingered in the sky.

A track seemed to open, as though it had not existed before we'd stared at the motor birds. It was fifty feet away, leading north towards the valley head and the source of the cry.

Sal reached into the car and emerged with his gun. We both had one: it was like a patrol. He started loping towards the T-junction track.

'Hey, Sal.'

He stopped, looked back at me.

I propped myself against the door. 'No way.'

'That fucking track is only six foot wide, man.'

'You don't walk out on a fare.'

We stood holding limp guns and staring bleakly. The progress of the day paused. When he walked back towards the car, it moved on.

'Look, if that's Spray playing games up there, I think I druther drop in unannounced. How 'bout if I go take a look and you stay here?' He looked doubtfully at me. I shook my head.

'I paid for this car and I wanna use it. Besides, it has bullet-resistant windows.'

'How resistant we don't know, I said that.'

'The engine runs quiet, too. We can creep up. They may not even see us – who's expecting a chauffeur service round here?'

He drew back the lips from his teeth and studied me, vexed but paralyzed.

'You're the driver,' I murmured and brushed my eyes downwards in the direction of the wheel.

The car went well on the trail: there was volcanic sand and patches of grass and flat shale and chippings and areas of smooth, bare rock.

'It's a *good* trail,' I said.

We got out and did some more listening half a mile in. We were on the side of the screaming hill, but the screams had gone. It was urgently still. Animal-land was taking siesta. Plant life was infinitely slowly growing. We didn't seem to count.

The smell was that much more noticeable. A wind might have carried it off. Noise might have distracted us. But the sun seemed to press it down and distribute it, like a spirit. A sick kind of kitchen smell, faint, as if it were permeating up into a bedroom. A smell like the rotting afterbirth of screams. It made Sal rear his head up like a hunting dog on a scent. I was already looking the way his snout pointed.

It moved us forward, away from the car.

There seemed to be light playing in the trees a hundred yards away up the slope, as if the brow of the hill was broken by a gulley against the sky. Walking on, across a glade of snowdrop-type winter flowers, it turned into reflections of water. But it wasn't that either. Sal had got ahead of me: he stopped first. It got clearer for me as I laboured up behind him, and I stopped as well.

Thirty yards away, the cork and green oak trees made a clearing under the shade of a towering kiawa tree. Strung twenty feet high from one of its boughs was a billowing teepee made of a white parachute.

Those were the facts, but pale smoke like a mist was wafting out from under the fringes of it, and the silk panels billowed ever so gently in a shaft of sun, so that it looked more like the battle tent of a Wagnerian god. Except for the reek.

We were braced in firing postures, ready to blast the shit out of anything that moved.

Sal muttered: 'No way anything's alive in there.'

Both of us frowning. Why a fire? The hill had hidden the smoke, but it was at least seventy degrees in the shade and eighty in the sun: who needed it? And who could survive in a wigwam with no chimney slot? Or in that smell?

We moved forward again, guns erect, working from one tree trunk to another.

Then we were at the pine-needle clearing, under the evergreen cool spread, and the parachute hung close, staked out with lengths of cord to six rough pegs. A couple of sunbeams were playing across it. It was almost beautiful. Smoke was running subtle wave-motion shadows across the silky fabric from inside. And there was another shape too, which jarred, unflowing, fixed, like the shadow of the smell.

I limped the dozen paces to a flap in the parachute panels and looked in.

The fire was a wide heap of ashes and charred embers, giving off a flue of pungent vapour which had filled the glinting space and which immediately attacked my eyes, but did not prevent me from identifying clearly what was strung over the fire, dangling by a ten-foot length of chain from the peak of the teepee. It was a man, strung up by the ankles like a freshly shot game bird, his arms flung wide like useless wings and his head making a slight pendulum swing a few feet above the heart of the glow. At first I thought he was swaddled in wet rags. I craned forward. The dark mess all over him was smoked blood, and the apparent strips of fabric – gashes in the flesh, hundreds of them. The sight sent a claw down into my gullet and scooped out the contents, which had already been well churned. They were bitter, inadequate and left a long salival land line from the ground to the corners of my mouth. I was wiping them away with the back of my gun hand when Sal made an incoherent noise behind me.

He barged rudely by and threw himself towards the fire, which would have instantly stripped his face and hands of flesh if I hadn't slapped him away with my elbow so that he fell inches short. Had he fainted? No, he'd fallen too hard.

I pivoted, aiming the gun, but the silk wafted across my face, a shadow reared behind it and something brutally decisive hit my brow.

25

LIKE I said, what with my leg wound, risking getting shot again had seemed like an option, so now I was willing to settle for being punched on the head: I lay down. The hardest thing was letting go of the gun. I ought to have got an Oscar for it – but a man knocked out cold would not hang on to an automatic. Still, I only dropped it a foot or two away. It was nice to be lying down, even with the smell, and my eyes scalding.

'Mickey!' Pause. 'Mickey!'

A second voice: 'He's fucked.'

'No! He's gotta pulse! A great pulse! Mickey!' – *slap!* – 'Mickey!'

'Leave 'im alone, Peekay. He's a mess.'

Just the two of them.

'What're you talking about? He's unconscious, that's all. Little bit of smoke inhalation, but you can't avoid that. It's penetrated the cuts excellently.'

'This goddamn reek is gonna make me throw up. And I hurt my knuckles. Whadda I do with these pair a dildos?'

'Take a look at them first . . . Mickey!'

'Uh, this explains the limo. It's the guy ran the Pooka Shell at Waimea Bay. Does chauffeur work onna side.'

'*He* could be dead, the way you chopped him.'

Mocking echo. 'Nah, he's unconscious, that's all. Nice weapon for a driver.'

'Mickey, you're going to pull through this' – *slap* – 'Mickey! I need you!'

144

'Cut him down, Peekay. It's disgusting.'

'Ever seen major surgery?'

'That's what he's gonna need. Shit, I'm gonna fetch up. Hey, Mr Tourist himself. Whadda I do with *him*?'

The voice indicated that he wasn't facing me. I took a look and it was the same curly mop I'd tangled with when I went botanizing – Einstein, the man Sal called Belkin Spray. He was wearing blue swimming goggles. And he still had his jean-jacket collar turned up. The man called Peekay I couldn't see. He was over my head on the other side of the fire. I heard him slapping the smoked man again.

'Mickey! Snap out of it!'

·'Knockiddoff, Peekay! Whadda I do with the spook?'

After a pause, the other voice said musingly: 'We'll talk to him.'

'Up the office?'

'I may need more wood.'

'Uppada office, Peekay?'

'Huh? Yes, try to revive him.'

It was my turn for some face-slapping, but I was out cold. Spray had to hoist me over his shoulder in a fireman's lift. While he was hauling me up I took a risk and lurched over so I could get back my gun. The other man was too busy with Mickey to notice. Sal lay sprawled out, breathing but out of it. There could have been a chance then, but a one-legged man risked being candidate number two for a naked roast. I hung limply over Belkin Spray's jean-jacket shoulder trailing my arms against his oily pants, with an automatic trained on his heel. Then I almost really lost consciousness: the smell in the tent mingled with a noseful of Belkin Spray's body odour was enough to knock out a mule.

Maybe two men my size would have made him stagger: with me up he walked easily out of the tent – *the air!* – and across to what I could see upside down past his waist was a military-issue pickup: it was army green with a forces license plate and a yellow diamond clipped to the fender. When he swung me round I lobbed the Japanese automatic under the front wheels.

Spray propped me against the fender and went away, leaving me facing the teepee, which was still floating on a cloud. I took out my wads of money, stacked them together and groped with them under the pickup's fender. Blindly, I found a wedging place, somewhere between the radiator and the grille. Footsteps came back and warm water was slopped over my head. I moaned realistically and put a hand to the bruise on my brow – wrong move! An ungoggled Spray stepped past me, grabbed the wrist, wrenched it behind my back, rolled me to one side, and coupled it with the other wrist I owned, cinching a plastic bracelet around the pair so that I was well trussed. Goodbye weapon. Goodbye upper limbs. Hello searing pain in the leg and in my bruised wrists. Then he frisked me.

It didn't get any better on the ride. I played the man who was too racked with pain to speak, could only slump against the cabin and groan: ninety per cent of my performance was genuine. The other ten per cent was me deeking out at Spray and up the trail to see where the hell we were headed. It was good to get clear of the barbecue in the teepee, but Sal was back there with a madman. And were we going towards, or away from Peppi Harman? I badly wanted to ask Belkin Spray, but I preferred him believing I was half dead.

With me trying to find a painless position for three of my limbs we drove wordlessly over the next spine of foothills, and crossed another forest valley into the lee of a steep mountain that was part of the main Koolau range. We came to a red and white boom across the trail with a plain wooden sentry box beside it. Before I could figure what was happening, a tawny-uniformed black MP in snow-white helmet and gloves stepped out and worked the boom so we didn't even have to slow down.

Spray pumped the wheel and threw us onto a steep trail which headed up the side of the mountain. Every couple of hundred yards it U-turned and I moaned. Soon we were getting views of the foothills and the Waianae mountains on the other side of the island. The barracks and Wheeler air-force base were huddled in the centre of the valley, defended by mountains to east and west. I pictured Oahu as above all an island fortress, the tourism only a sideline confined to a stockade called Waikiki. That I was riding manacled in a military vehicle with a reeking actor freak made as much sense as anything else. Getting waved on by an

MP in wedding gloves after quitting the grotesquerie in the parachute capped it.

We rounded an outcrop and beheld the transporter planes circling overhead, big aluminium freighter birds so close you could see the oil slicks on their engine cowlings. Then they were gone, disappearing over the summit that was only a mile away now, with a white pod standing near it on land that was almost bare.

We emerged from the woods, and the trail snaked ahead through scrub and rocks up to the pod. It could have been a modified Cape Cod lighthouse. It had a white dome on top like a revolving observatory, with a smaller cylinder standing beside it, linked by a bridge, possibly for a siderostat. There were familiar hirsute characters from Spray's team of associates standing guard near the doors and beside a familiar vehicle which was parked on the forecourt. I blinked half-shut eyes: it was the '52 Ford pickup, and it was badly damaged round the snout, which proved that I had indeed been rammed. My head went into a spin. I could have confirmed my car's damage from the renta-wreck people. But that assumed they'd reclaimed. Lau had probably impounded it. The greasy lawman's espionage accusation rankled me afresh, and I thought of Ilsa's head being colonized by flies in the well of her Volkswagen.

A horn blaring behind us interrupted my glowering thoughts. Spray ignored it, but while he looked away I grabbed a retroglance at a brown military GM staff car kicking up a plume near the tree line.

We parked on the forecourt before a wide vista of the island. Spray got out and lit a butt. When the staff car drew up alongside us at the pod, Sal got out, caught my eye across the car roof and gave me an expression that embraced the damage to the limo, his separation from it, the bruise on his neck and the lingering horror of the teepee. I tried to show I was glad to see him.

Spray came round and opened my door. Sal helped me out with manacled hands.

'This fruit just offered me a job,' he murmured by my face as I stepped down. 'Where's my gun?'

Spray pulled him away from the truck and slammed the door. 'Button up, Shanks. This whut yer lookin' fer?' The tedious business end of Sal's revolver came out and spoiled the view. It took some spoiling. We were on a true summit, with a prospect of the dreaming Pacific in three directions. Only the Waianae mountains blocked the seascape to the west. The drone of the orbiting transporters cast a snoring laziness across the hills a mile or two to the south.

Spray's boss came up to me. Two more different men would have been hard to imagine. Spray was like something that walked off a he-man movie set: this man had walked straight out of – not a teepee where a bleeding man was strung over a bonfire – but a boutique on Cañon Boulevard, Beverly Hills. He was only an inch or two shorter than me, well made with sleek features and soft, sandy hair brushed back off a high, tanned forehead. The sweater was subtle blue-gray alpaca, with the sleeves pulled up from honey-coloured forearms sprinkled with golden hairs and equipped with a wafer-thin timepiece and chunky gold bracelet; the slacks were knife-edged navy twills, the gray suede loafers Gucci-looking with brass buckles. Everything was crisply Holmby Hills except the eyes. They reminded me of Dr Petreen's just after she'd shot me. Very controlled, but patently dangerous.

'How d'you do, Mr Wallace? You seem better,' he said. Sal looked back at me with resignation, leaning on the hood of the staff car with his bound hands. I mugged to show forgiveness. 'Mr Spray,' he said, keeping the expression of bright fury on me, 'kindly remove the cuffs, they aren't required. Are they?'

I tried out a shrug but I was already strapped into a half-shrug, so it didn't work. Spray approached me holding a machete-size bowie. The steel was cold between my thumb pads, then circulation was rushing painfully back into my hands. Spray cut Sal loose and stood fitting the knife back into its sheath at his hip, watching for me to rub life back into my wrists, but I wasn't going to give him the pleasure. I let them hang, throbbing.

'Prospero and Caliban,' I said. Spray's cragged face came up at that. The little eyes glinted with something like amusement. The stubble round his mouth twisted into a leer.

'The *right* Duke of Milan, you will recall,' the man in alpaca said suavely. I kept quiet. He slapped his pockets in a let's-get-weaving way. 'Well!' He glanced at Sal, who looked blank. 'I gather we've been labouring under a misapprehension about you,

Mr Wallace. According to Sal here you spend far too high a proportion of your visits to Hawaii in his bar to be engaged in any sort of espionage. Are we to believe that?'

This got my goat. I stabbed an aching thumb over my shoulder.

'Can you tell me what I was looking at back there?'

'Hmmm, yes,' he said, frowning slightly, as if I'd committed a delicate social gaffe. 'I'm afraid radical alternative medicine can be as messy as the conventional kind.'

I blurted: 'How come Ilsa Regner is dead in her car at the stables?' And pointing at the actor, stormed: 'Did you finish her, Spray? Because if you did, so help me, I'll see you pay for it.'

The spurt of pent-up outrage had me choking, but I cooled off some when I saw their wary incomprehension. The man in Gucci loafers turned to Spray with a puzzled expression. Caliban shrugged.

'Are you saying that somebody has died at the stables, Mr Wallace?'

The question hung in the air as the drone of aero-engines laid its timelessness across the afternoon.

'Look,' I said. 'Who the fuck *are* you?' I groped around like an orchestral maestro: the pod, the vehicles, Belkin Spray, the boutique clothes, the view, the teepee back in the foothills . . . 'What *is* all this?'

There was a second during which no spoken answer came, only a kind of shiver that seemed to animate Spray's boss into replying.

'My name is Rayner, Mr Wallace. Philip Keith Rayner. People call me Peekay.'

'Any relation to P. K. Rayner?'

'That's me. You probably mean my grandfather of the same name. He founded the chain of stores. Of course we've diversified since then, but nobody's ever leveraged the critical mass, it remains closely held. And the name still lends a certain, how shall we say, kudos?'

He was steering me by the arm towards the pod. One of Spray's henchmen eased out of the small entrance door and stood beside it like a sentry. He was a thickset Latino type with a crossbreed Afro and his jean suit was lumpy and oil soaked.

Two Filipino urchins were behind the pickup, astride their burp-bikes, watching me sullenly.

We went in, climbed turning stairs, walked a couple of galleries, mounted more stairs and entered a small, round cathedral dedicated to the god astronomy. The area was open, with a raised framework in the centre bracketed onto an enormous horseshoe mounting. We walked under grille-work galleries, past gray metal desks with beige computer terminals crouching on them.

'All very impressive and way beyond my means, I can assure you,' P. K. Rayner said, guiding me into a partitioned area laid out like a government office, with a metal desk against one wall, an assortment of folding metal chairs and a kitchenet with table in the corner. He waved at an imposing console which reminded me of recording studio controls. 'They work it all from there on the rare occasions our man-made troposphere still allows it,' he said, reaching under the steel desk and producing a bottle of rye and two lowball glasses.

I took the drink, noting that Belkin Spray and Sal had not followed us. I refused the seat he indicated. He sat down in a swivel chair by the desk, which had a couple of cordless phones lying on it. The whiskey helped me stand more steadily. I took the bottle and poured out some more.

'Well?' Rayner said briskly, squaring up on me, the man in charge of things, with an eerie light in his eyes.

For a second I balked. We were in an advanced astronomical-cum-communications installation on military land. It was being guarded by unemployed actors, and the golf-kart type apparently in charge was the heir to a department store chain. It seemed appropriate to invoke my citizenship and demand to see the commanding officer, but my neck hairs were tingling, I was too hot on the scent.

'I'm looking for Peppi Harman,' I said.

'Why?'

'That mean you know who she is?'

'I may do.'

'D'you know *where* she is?'

'It depends.'

I conquered a sudden weakness in my good leg.

'So you know where she is.'

'Like I said, it depends.'

'What on?'

'Why are you looking for her?'

I almost blurted the reason. Instead, I heard myself say: 'I am the family's architect, a legal executor of her father's will.'

'So?'

'We have to establish that she's alive.'

'I see.'

'Where is she?'

Rayner said lightly: 'She's a guest at my home.'

Feeling queerly unreal, I replied: 'Here?'

'Hardly here.' He waved in the direction of the control console, the computers beyond, and the arcane erection aimed at the dome.

'Where then?'

He stared brilliantly at me, rigid with pent-up excitement. I stared back, searching for meaning. After a long pause during which he appeared to be suppressing the passion bottled up in him, he got up and walked to the single small window set three feet into the curved wall. After looking out of it twisting his fingers for a few moments, he turned to me and said: 'I am dying of Aids. It has taken a long time for me to be able to say it as simply as that. Over a year, to be precise.'

The words settled coldly over the spare furnishings of the room. I said nothing. Parts of the kaleidoscope in my head were shifting, connecting where I was to where I had been, giving form to my wounds and shape to the journey. After a moment the movement of the pattern brought me back to my question and I asked it: 'Where is Peppi?'

'If you'll bear with me, I'll come to that,' Rayner said. 'You see, I feel more alive now than ever in my life – and yet I'm dying. Ironic, isn't it. My family helped to build California. I control great wealth. When I was given a sudden death sentence, I was enraged, and I swore to buy a reprieve. But as you may know, there is no conventional cure.' He turned and went to his drink, sipped it and looked up at an iron bookcase packed with folders. 'I bought into thirty corporations around the world, but I'm afraid all their treatments were expensive exercises in flimflammery, and the prospects of any real advance, if there were any, postdated my death by many years, if not decades.' He dismissed the shelves of documents with a motion of his drink. 'There's millions on paper in there. I decided recently that nothing would come of it all.'

He held out his glass and I poured it half full of whiskey. Confiding in me, his eyes had deepened, losing the manic glaze.

'Put some soda in it, would you,' he said. 'Have to watch myself.' I topped him up from the siphon. He sank onto the rim of the desk and took a gulp. 'Then my denial phase wore off and I realized that I was finished,' he went on. 'And you know? It cut me loose. The whole thing moved onto a new level for me. I abandoned the laboratories and got out of California. I'd had everything in life. Now fate was forcing something really huge on me.' He opened his arms with a mischievous grin. 'I had to find the cure *myself*!'

I said: 'So the scene down there – '

He broke in sharply: 'That is a very radical experiment which I would never have performed if I didn't believe a major breakthrough was *very* close.' He was on his feet again now, with the strutting self-confidence filling him out. I could hear him calling across the acrid smoke and sickly-sweet stench of fried flesh, *Mickey, Mickey*. 'I am tapping some unexplored sources of totally alternative medicine,' he said.

The pattern jerked convulsively across my head and let in a name: I called it out.

'Regner!'

He bucked his eyebrows and nodded with a keen little smile.

'It was your people raiding his papers,' I breathed.

He continued evenly: 'I went back to the theory that monkeys were the origin. I believe it means there is nothing new in this world and that Aids has occurred before.'

'Primitive medicine.'

'*Ancient* medicine,' he corrected. 'From South America, Polynesia, Asia, Australia – yes, and Africa itself. Forget Darwin, men have inhabited this planet for millions of years. Everything has come and gone before, *including Aids*! It is a matter of *re*discovering the cure!'

'And Regner – '

'Regner did very important work in Fiji in the late 1920s. He self-published one book which was ignored, but it is a mine of anecdotes about practices which had already died out. His private papers contain much more material.' He stopped pacing about and confronted me, hands reaching out. 'How could I wait for Regner to die and let some ridiculous arboretum lock away his papers for years until some PhD hack butchered them?'

'Why didn't you ask the guy,' I blazed back.

'Because his fucking wife's a spy!' he shouted.

I stood there feeling as if I'd been lammed with a bat. Rayner turned away and raged at the walls.

'When I threw millions at the labs nobody gave a flying damn. The day I take the thing on myself everybody and his brother is after me, and why? For the fucking *money!*'

'But Ilsa Regner wasn't after money,' I said.

His head came round. The eyes were wild, the voice brittle.

'She had no choice. Forget perestroika. The Soviets are more desperate for money than ever before. East bloc people controlled her from way back. They still use all the methods. She probably had family in the gulags.'

'So you had Spray kill her.'

'No!'

'Then who did?'

He walked to his drink and sipped it.

'Mr Wallace,' he said. 'Do you have the faintest conception of the revenues that would come from a patented treatment for the disease that is killing me?'

'Did she know?'

'She had access to Regner's papers. If, as you say, she was murdered near the stables, she might have witnessed the experiment and died because of her knowledge. It was only a couple of miles away, I had to work outside military property. My status as a general in the national guard allows me to rent this obsolete observatory to experiment with cosmic bombardment, but I'd be pushing my luck if I smoked men over Sinoo Nganga wood on Uncle Sam's property. There, now you've got the secret, interested in making a few thousand million dollars?'

'Cosmic bombardment?' I echoed.

An oily, Hawaiian-Chinese accented voice which I recognized said from the doorway behind me: 'Raise your hands and keep them where I can see them, please.'

26

A SHIELD made a brief appearance.

'Lieutenant Lau, Honolulu PD.'

Rayner went rigid.

A man with a sawn-off tuft atop his head and horn-rimmed glasses pegging up a blue business suit came in behind Lau, hidden from Rayner. A deep crevice divided the top of his face.

'Well, well, Hedwig Maronek,' I said. Rayner remained rigid, and lost more colour. He seemed to snap bone cartilage to force himself forward into a posture of conviction.

'This is Federal property,' he barked with some generalship, but Lau only strode towards him, gun outstretched like an Olympic torch and rapid-fired him twice in the face so close that the wall behind went blotched red with a splashy noise.

P. K. Rayner's arms were thrown up in a death surrender by the rat-tat impact and he hit the ground like a fallen punchbag, staring cross-eyed up at two holes in his brow, a halo of it spreading onto the floor.

The bottleneck in my trembling right hand was suddenly electric. Lau had his arm outstretched, gun smoking over his victim in a tableau of triumph and destruction. It gave me the half-second required to loop the bottle over onto his skull at right angles, neatly between the parietal and the occipital. The bottle held, the cranium gave, the lying cop went down, firing his automatic twice more.

With great professionalism Maronek the security expert kept his weapon trained on my sternum while he looked down shaken at his dead employer and the unconscious policeman. Our eyes met and communicated the reflex brotherhood of survivors. We were both deafened, and sudden death had neutralized our egos. Two disturbed animals tacitly agreed to live on – for now.

'Where's Spray and Sal and the others?' I asked across the aural whiteout.

He glanced down again, dragged his eyes from the floor and gave me a keen look. 'Arrested. Outside with the other faggots,' he said.

'So this was supposed to be a legitimate operation,' I said, and checked the bottle. Centrifugal force had not driven all the whiskey out of it, there was a good three inches left. One of the most powerful bottles of Jim Beam ever manufactured: I drank from it. More did I never need a drink.

Maronek reached into his inside pocket and showed the top of a folded legal document.

'Mr Rayner was dismissed as Chief Executive and voted off the board at 10 am Pacific time,' he advised. 'I'm here as a representative of the corporation.'

'Kind of a radical dismissal,' I said, surveying the dead scenery, with its vividly widening pool of poisoned blood.

'He went for his gun, you saw it,' Maronek said. 'There won't be any postmortem.'

'No inquest?'

'Take a look round. This whole setup is proof of insanity. Lau did a great job. Arresting Spray and his crowd – or most of them – without a shot fired was an inspiration to watch.'

'Sure. The blond fellow is my chauffeur.'

'He was. You're going to jail.'

The gunfire adrenalin had set me simmering. The chutzpah of Hedwig Maronek made me boil. His ringingly clear idea of who was going to jail defied the giant heaps of guilt stacked up around the room.

'Lau's in line for a big reward,' he said, looking down at the hero, who was stirring.

'He's a bent cop,' I said. 'Find out who killed Ilsa Regner. You need a bucket of water and keep him awake for at least twelve hours. How's Jayne, your live-in ladyfriend? Did she sort it out with Dr Petreen about that little medical problem?'

He kept the gun so steadily on me it could have been gyro-controlled. 'Very funny,' he said, and glanced down again. He wanted to help Lau. His expression indicated the unspoken survival deal we'd had was almost off.

'How can I be shot resisting arrest if you don't have power to arrest?' I asked. 'It'd be murder. The deputies outside would stand witness. You may've been a cop once, but you're a company dick now, not one of them.'

Maronek was impervious. He said: 'They've left,' and added shrewdly: 'Did Mr Rayner tell you where Penelope is?'

'Sure,' I said. 'He's got her hidden. Had her.'

Maronek nodded. 'Yeah, the day Pete Harman had his accident he locked her up. She was staying on with Spray and the gang and Mr Rayner tucked her in his back pocket as an insurance policy.'

'Because you were leaning on him.'

Maronek shrugged. 'Ec-c-ch, he let me handle things pretty much my way after we'd had a talk about his health. Bad for the company image, his condition.'

'Isn't it your condition, too? Why else would you try to inject me with your own blood?'

'I'm not president and CEO, and I'm not full-blown. He was.' Maronek indicated the draining corpse with his gun barrel. 'Lau did the guy a favour.'

'What about peddling skag out of the company drugstores? What kind of condition's that?'

'Like you say, we had an understanding about it.'

'But you aim to retire now. With Jayne. On the Harman fortune.'

He split a crooked smile. 'How can I? He died intestate. Peppi Harman's still alive.'

'You knew that when you fixed her father.'

The security man smirked. 'Pete Harman didn't get it because anybody wanted the money *off* him. They didn't want him giving it *away*.'

'Who to?'

Maronek inclined his sawn-off cranium. 'Him.' He indicated the door. 'Walk or you're dragged out,' he said.

'What for?' I answered. He looked blank and nudged air with the gun. 'What was Pete Harman giving Rayner the money *for*?' I repeated.

The pause that followed, and the incomprehension on the beefy face, convinced me that Maronek had his ham hands full with dope turnover and the Harman inheritance and no more.

'Some dumb foundation for dying fags,' he said. 'Petreen got real keen when she found out 'bout my HIV pos.'

'So all you got to do is rub out the girl,' I said.

He smirked.

'And live it up for the time I got left, which is fine by me. Now move, and remember, I got nothin' to lose.'

Lau stirred again, and grunted. It took no great brains to talk Maronek's language and act like one of the family.

'Listen, Pete turned me on,' I said. 'There's a fix in my pocket, let me use it before I go.'

His lip twisted with a nasty familiarity.

'Needle punk, huh?'

I took it as permission, put the Jim Beam down on the desk beside me and reached into the inside pocket of my chino jacket for the Ray-Ban case where I had stashed Pete Harman's outfit. It was an outfit that looked like a billion others, the sort that wash up free on Long Island beaches, frosty plastic disposable, made by Ortho.

'Miracle shit,' I murmured, throwing the jacket aside and fumbling with my left shirt cuff.

Here's how Hedwig Maronek's mind worked: he kept a firearm trained on me during Rayner's summary execution and an assault on Lau with a deadly bottle and an assault on himself with deadly insult but when I bent over preparing to shoot up, he let the barrel go down and point at the black vinyl floor.

After switching the fit, my right fist had the bottle arcing up under the bridge of his nose before he could rectify his error with the gun. He fired at the floor, and his septum gristle made a noise buckling. Shards of it were probably forced into his cerebellum: his legs buckled under him before he could aim or fire again, and the gun polkaed away.

I righted the bottle quickly to save the dregs and stood it back on the desk, then I trod on Maronek's left palm, bent down and exposed enough wrist to find a vein. After I'd emptied the cylinder I rubbed the trace with my thumb, massaging upwards towards the heart. I stepped across him and flung the fit through an air-duct grille.

The dome room was deserted. There was nobody in the galleries on the way down, or out on the forecourt. Impossible to hide Spray, Sal, the boys, the sentry and enough arresting officers in the Ford pickup, the US Army Toyota or the GM staff car. Apparently Lau's men had obeyed orders to cut out of Federal territory while the going was good. From far behind me came the distinctive clatter of one of the metal stacking chairs in Rayner's office falling over. I thought of the cordless phones on the desk.

The Toyota looked sweet and precious. I scooped a hand under the front fender and groped round the wall of the radiator. The bible of money was wedged there. I brought it out, looked at it, then reached under again and put it back.

It was the gasoline model, with good acceleration, and it handled well on the switchback down the mountain. I got waved through the checkpoint with wedding gloves, a mark of initiation.

It seemed a long way.

The limousine had gone. But the teepee was still there, still floating on a cloud.

Holding my breath, I cut Mickey down by holding an ember against the blue nylon rope which bound his ankles to the chain. As it smouldered, I made a pendulum of him and he came down on the fourth swing towards me, which tested my skill at hopping sideways fast. There was no way I could help him without water or without touching the congealed blood. I sucked some less foul air from outside, poked my mouth at his ear and muttered urgently: 'Mickey, we're going to kill P. K. Rayner. Where does he live?'

My ear hovered over his scorched face.

'Black Point,' Mickey whispered faintly back through the cracked lips.

Revenge is that rotten.

27

BLACK POINT. The Cap d'Antibes of Hawaii. In the crook of the bay, halfway along the promontory, a money-crazed Moorish palace built in the 1930s by heiress Doris Duke, overlooking endless rollers. Other rich spreads scattered around. Palms waving everywhere like fistfuls of dollars.

My first bet for the location of Rayner's house was the headland, which was inside a private estate – unmarked, naturally. I approached the guard at the gate driving my calling card. He came alongside. I pulled my jacket over my leg and pumped the window.

'Hi.' Keep it simple, nothing to hide. 'I'm the new guy. The Rayner place?'

He had a swatch of corn hair falling from under his cap band, and a pair of buck teeth falling from his lip. The eyes were knowing.

'You guys cleaning up the act, huh?'

He thought his tan security uniform and shoulder lanyard hooked him into the High Command. We were supposed to be mess-hall buddies. I grinned wryly.

'I guess Spray and his crowd got too much pomade on the upholstery.'

The leer intensified.

'Plenty else besides, huh?'

I let it ride, a busy man. He dropped it and backed off.

'Fork right, it's the last house. Called Day-lease.' He went back to his desk, where I glimpsed him opening *Hustler* magazine like a pair of thighs.

There were no houses, only a couple of baronial portals a hundred yards apart and lots of mature foliage being rustled by the warm sea breeze.

Rayner owned the end of Black Point: there was a twelve-foot brown-brick bulwark stretching away each side of a gateway about twenty-foot high, roofed over in pagoda style. On wooden louvres over the studded wooden entrance gates was a wrought-iron sign: *Délice*. Palm trees hung over the bricks and waved. They were the only welcome: there was no bell pull, no press-button, no handles, no knobs, it was like Jericho on battle day.

Pressure can inspire you. I went to the pickup and pressed the glove compartment. It opened. Inside, on top of a stack of handbooks, was a gadget made of black plastic. It resembled the remote control of a video recorder except it had only one rocker button. I got in, closed the pickup door, leaned out and pointed the thing at the gates, squeezed. Nothing. The gates reared up a few feet taller. Two squeezes and wait. Think about nothing else. Concentrate . . . Look at the gadget again: maybe it's Spray's pager. No, a humming noise, something moved. The gates opening. I pushed the shift and eased forward.

A paved drive bordered with banana plants and monster cacti curved down and away, no residence in sight. It curved back again, then levelled out and led onto a wide parking apron. The view said: I Own the World. It was ocean, then Molokai and Maui, mistily dreaming, then infinity.

The facade of the house which filled the south and west was Shinto-brutal. Long blocks of Asian hardwood four-foot broad and thick had been stacked up to make a double story. The roof was tiled with six-inch lozenges of rock. There was a moat with pink and white lilies crossed by a wooden gangway to an entrance marked by three steep outcrops of juggernaut timber. Nothing so banal as a window showed in the puzzle of slots in the wall.

I parked overlooking the ocean and checked for a way round the upended lumber, but the place teetered over the breaking surf below, landscaped onto a hundred-yard-long ledge. A gulley going down to the sand was lined with coils of razor wire. I limped back and crossed the footbridge. In a porch under the mass of timber was a rockpool fed by a waterfall. Fat carp and goldfish meandered boredly in the gloom. The door was cased in solid copper with businesslike brass bolts set in crisscross patterns. Overhead, swathes of pea-green foliage swooped out of nowhere. I held out the gadget and squeezed three times. Nothing, only the sound of water.

A few paces back, on the gangway, the stacked chunks of Sumatran ecology gave me a clue. Every brutalistic cleft and crevice was a foothold. My moccasin pumps weren't the ideal footwear, and my left leg had to be a passenger for the right but the climb was elementary enough for it not to matter. And once I got over the eaves and onto the roof it would be like walking up a hill.

It took only a few moments to get up onto the stone roof slabs. I crawled up to the ridge and peeked over at the backyard of a god. A bathing-pool-cum-ornamental lagoon worthy of the Taj Mahal stretched away to a pagoda made of more milled forest and quarried crag. Three soaring date palms, as tall and erect as navy flagpoles, stood in front of it. Away to the south and west was a poem of ocean, with turquoise breakers wasting themselves on white sand.

The house had a wing excavated into the hillside. Staggered terraces connected it to the ornamental lagoon. On the nearest an array of plump recliners was ranged round a portable bar unit in chrome and glass, and a polished, low-slung glass table. Shade was supplied by a timber pergola draped with strands of rambling rose coming into leaf. Peppi was standing with her back to the wing, looking below me into the house. She had on a blue Brazilian-cut monokini and was holding a towel bunched up to her chest.

'*Peppi!*'

She reacted, looked up, making a vizor with her hand.

'Cody? Is that you?' The husky bell voice carried so that I could have been standing in front of her. Carried a load of alarm and discomfort, too.

I put my hands on the roof ridge.

'Rayner's been shot,' I said. 'Let's go. I've got an army vehicle. It'll get us to the harbour. We'll get help later. Got to get off the island. Right now.'

'Cody . . .' *Looking into the house underneath me. Not budging.* 'You shouldn't've come here.' Peering up again. 'You look terrible.'

'Peppi, we gotta move!'

Running her hand through her hair: 'Oh, shit!'

'And better grab a gun, y'know where he keeps them?'

'Oh God, Cody. I can't come with you.' Bowing her head, biting into a knuckle, looking towards the house. I stared hard at the roof, but eyes don't see through six-inch rock.

Our heads jerked at the same time when we caught the uproar of a tortured engine and screeching tyres bursting through the soundproof wall of the estate onto the drive.

She turned and hurried away, up steps, across a higher terrace into the other wing of the house, disappearing through a pair of open French doors.

I rolled over and pinned my back against the pitch of the roof. Rayner's army staff car careened out of the trees and slewed to a halt on the forecourt. Lau emerged pulling a weapon out of his belt, took in the Toyota pickup and hurried towards the porch below me.

Peppi came out onto the drive near the trees wearing a thigh-length T-shirt and white espadrilles. She glanced back towards Lau's car and started running up the drive.

'Hey, *Lau!*'

The black head reappeared, moving across the footbridge onto the forecourt, swivelling back and forth as the gun barrel raked the facade of the house.

I slithered crabwise down the pitch of the roof, building up more speed than I could handle, but on track to jump him. Near the brink, irrevocably committed to the leap, I glimpsed the pockmarked disc with its puffy eyes whipping round and upwards, the mouth an 'O'.

There was a familiar scream from the driveway and a flash of white fabric and frizzy apricot hair. The head snapped towards her, the gun tracking after it. Lau scuttled out of my path and took aim. I could see the bead he had on her: she blazed high white against the background, running towards me. Out of control, I logrolled over the eaves into free fall.

The pistol blast raised a wild mewing among the gulls. After

I hit water something harder than water pounded me into a place where I could hear the echo of the shot bouncing off all the landmarks, one by one, from Diamond Head to the Koolau range, then down through cold rock into the underworld. All Hawaii flowed through me in a dark river . . .

28

I WOKE up not knowing whether I'd heard ambulance sirens or Hawaiian ghosts keening for their vanished nation. Round the edge of my vision a frieze of palm heads brushed the sky. I lay and let an uncaring mid-Pacific afternoon juggle its fragrances of sandalwood, eucalyptus and salt against the blue. I thought: if I let go, I drift back again into where Peppi's been blasted to. Life seemed to want me, though; I couldn't figure why. I turned away from it and looked down into the deep, where Peppi'd gone.

There was a hawking cough. A big woman was standing by the waterfall. She had a flaring mane of tawny hair, jet-black upside-down glasses, a smouldering Long in her mouth, and she wore a heavily filled swooping V-neck white sweater and black slacks. She removed the butt and spat accurately in the moat.

Somebody had dragged my body out of the water and laid it on the boardwalk in a puddle like a thing dredged up.

Jayne Harman, a.k.a. Maronek, took a deep suck at her cigaret and spoke in vapours. 'Lucky for you there's no piranhas.'

I told my arms to jack me up onto my elbows. They had a try, but my left leg came out against it and my head went back down. I caned the arms and overruled the leg. It took some doing, but I got there. Then it was possible to roll over onto my side and push my torso upright. The leg objected, and forced a hissing noise out of my mouth. I needed a third hand to wipe the dripping hair away from my eyes but there wasn't one available.

'Have to see to that leg. Who shot you?'

My throat made as if to speak, and brought up a belch of pond water. I tried again.

'Your friend Dr Petreen – well, waddaya know.'

Dr Petreen came out of the shadows. She had on a pair of tight stonewashed Levis and a T-shirt with the motto: *Made in Japan*. Her troublesome black locks were pinned up in cute disarray. The pretty eyes were unscrambled and looking doctor at me.

I found them lifting an arm each and dragging. D-cups one side, snake bites the other, take yr choice.

Inside, they dumped me in a black cowhide studio chair. My clothes squelched as I lay back. We were in an atrium done out desert style: sand, cactuses and bleached wood. One side of the room was open onto a dappled rosewalk, with the ornamental lagoon beyond it and across the lagoon, lawns, a pillared parapet and the ocean. The two women stood looking down at me, breathing a bit. Petreen kneeled down and professionally undid my belt. I helped her get the pants down to my knees. She started in on my dressing with a pair of orange-handled kitchen scissors.

'What've they done with Peppi?' I asked.

Jayne Maronek removed the Long from her mouth and coughed. 'She's being taken care of.'

Things sank. Colour drained from the room.

'He'll be back,' I said. 'Me too he can shoot.'

'Should be interesting,' the Maronek woman said, sucking on the cigaret and blowing away smoke to the side. My eyes followed it.

Then I saw Lau.

He was stretched out like a piece of luggage, his hands folded over the central button of his terrible suit, the flat hamburger face almost childlike in deathly pallor.

I grabbed a fistful of pants and stood up like a man with two good legs.

'That's Lau.'

'So?' said Jayne Maronek.

'You nailed him.' A big twisted knot started loosening inside.

'She did.' Maronek cocked her head at Petreen, who kneeled modestly waiting to resume work on the dressing. 'Heard the car, grabbed a gun. Right when you shouted she had the door open. Had time to aim. Real surgical, in the heart. Self-defence. We called Hawaii P D.'

My head replayed the single shot ringing out as I fell. It made me dizzy.

'He shoot Peppi?'

'No, like I said, she's gone downtown to be looked after.'

I sank into the edge of the studio chair. Petreen started clipping close to my pinstripe boxer shorts.

'You come with Maronek?' My voice felt strangely light.

'Not exactly. I followed him – we followed him.'

Petreen made a guttural noise. The dressing lay open. The wound had made the top part of my leg angry. It was red with rage. With a yellow heart that smelled. She started bathing it with a pad dabbed with liquid from a bottle on the floor that made my teeth grind.

'Why?'

'Because he had Pete Harman killed.'

She reached out and crushed the cigaret against the trunk of a cactus, let it fall. She'd taken the glasses off and her eyes had the almost human expression I remembered from when she'd talked about the years spent living on a Mexican beach with a tormented young author called Pete Harman. How in spite of everything she'd refused to sign for his committal.

'And you figured he'd fix Peppi too.'

'He's so depressed he's reckless.'

'Depressed because he's sick?'

'Uh-huh.'

'With something he passed on to you.'

'No.'

'No?'

'She just called the lab in Palo Alto.'

Petreen didn't look up from swabbing. She said: 'We both lucked in.'

'Maronek's luck ran out,' I said. 'He's probably dead. Some kind of overdose. He's trying out the floor at a disused observatory Rayner'd got hold of in the mountains.' I left out my part in it.

168

Petreen gasped.

'That's too bad,' Jayne Maronek interjected dryly towards her. 'What happened, anyway?'

'Lau shot Rayner dead point-blank. Rayner had some wild idea about curing Aids with jungle medicine. The hideout's on army property, way up in the hills. Lau's interested in the profit side, along with some other people. At least, he was. Until you treated him, Doctor.'

My leg was stinging. Petreen patted the new dressing and stood up. I hoisted the slacks.

'Heddie was wise to Rayner's condition. He was blackmailing him,' she said.

Jayne Maronek glanced keenly at her. The smaller woman shrugged.

'He reinvested it in the business,' she said. 'I never saw any money.'

I said: 'I guess it was a nice setup. But basically peanuts compared with the Harman thing. It was big league, and legitimate. Trouble was, Pete Harman was insane and planned to give the dough away for the operation you told him about, Doctor – after you mentioned the possibility of reviewing his patient status and locking him up. I figure P. K. Rayner grabbed Peppi to keep Maronek quiet, which Maronek took for leaning on Pete. Then Spray passed on the news about granma's millions and it turned into more blackmail. Rayner was ending up as deranged as your Mr Maronek.'

'A death sentence can do that,' Petreen said thoughtfully, looking skew-eyed at me.

'It made sense stopping Pete, but I don't buy murder,' Jayne Maronek said.

'Squeamish about it, huh?' I came back. 'You could still stomach holding a gun on your daughter.'

The Maronek woman's eyes narrowed, glittering as she shook her head.

'Sure you could,' I cooed. 'Don't think 'cause I cracked my head on a rock out there I don't get the picture. When Lau turned up you had a gun on Peppi, I could see it in her eyes. What were you trying to do, make her sign a cheque to you and your new pal?'

Standing up was easier with the new dressing, although the pant leg hung in tatters. I looked round for the door. My colleague the architect hadn't made finding any doors easy. Only limitless money made this heap of logs easy.

Jayne Maronek barked out behind me: 'So you got a theory Peppi was being held here by Rayner when she telephoned me yesterday, huh?'

The words hit me in a queasy spot I'd avoided ever since hearing from Sal that she'd been seen at the riding stables. They reined me in on my way to the door and brought me round.

'What about it?'

'She was free as a bird, lover boy. When we got here earlier she was sunbathing in an empty house – wasn't she . . . ' Jayne Maronek kept watching me. She and Petreen were standing holding hands.

'The gates were wide open when our taxi got here,' Petreen said. 'When we got to the front door you could see the lagoon in back and the view of the ocean. Peppi was lying by the pool reading. It was *The End of Nature* by Bill McKibben. I remember because I'd just finished it myself. Of course, we shut everything and tried to talk her into getting away.'

Inside I was reeling, but I held my ground. I was on the roof looking over the ridge, watching Peppi dash for the wing of the house as Lau's car came through the gates I'd left open. I replayed her running out the other side of the house towards the drive and glancing back at the porch. The insight jabbed me back into the room.

'It was you she was escaping from, not Lau,' I insisted. 'I thought it was Lau, but he was after me.'

'Wrong again, mister,' Jayne Maronek drawled. 'I held no gun on her. I didn't need to. All I told her to do was write a will. A doctor is my witness.'

Hand in hand with her, Petreen was nodding, still cross-eyed.

'A will . . . ' I echoed, the queasy patch clawing outwards.

'Sure. Don't you get it yet? I told you when you came to my place last week. She used to run with Spray and his crowd at state college. They all worked Central Park that summer. It was before the scare really got going. Before people cleaned up their acts, right? When they got her up here they gave her a little piece of *bad news*. It kind of changed her attitude. You can bet it was Peppi called Pete and made up his mind on the donation – '

I swung round and made for the door. Sirens were mewing beyond the ridge.

' – and hey, lover boy, better forget about the wedding!'

The taunt snaked after me and curdled my vision as I hobbled across the front lot to the pickup.

A brown army staff car I recognized cut in front of me as I exited Black Point. The windows were suntanned, but I thought I glimpsed a silver pendant glinting among a cluster of black curls over the steering wheel as it passed.

Several sirens were making whoopee along the skirt of Diamond Head. I veered away from them and accelerated up the coast.

29

I CLEANED out the engine compartment, shunted the pickup over a cliff near Kahana Bay and thumbed a ride along the coast from a telephone repairman.

At the Robinson Crusoe cottage, her old Datsun was gone. The driftwood front doors were unlocked. The room smelt partly musty, partly overlayed with a fresh haze of 711 cologne. A T-shirt dress was flung across her bed and a pair of espadrilles lay on the rug. The shower stall was steamy, and the imminence of her being naked there made me ache. After I'd found a pencil and written a message on the back of a torn envelope I made a call to the limousine service and walked up to Highway 83 to thumb a ride. A pineapple trucker stopped for me.

When I found Hans Regner at home, he said he'd just been delivered back from a formal identification at the morgue by Sheriff Quilley. He was sitting in one of his cane chairs on the porch looking a hundred. He couldn't bring himself to talk about Ilsa, but he listened when I described Rayner's experimental operation, and the haze blew out of his eyes when I told him about Mickey.

'They had that out of *Fiji Floriensis*!' he wheezed, clambering out of his chair. 'God damn them! I quoted Dietrich Seelig on poison sinoo!' He tottered into his study, throwing away his stick with a curse, pulled down a fat reference work, riffled the pages, pinned one down and peered at it. '*Sinoo nganga!*' he went. '*Sinoo nganga! Excoecaria agallocha!* God damn the beggars, it was cited as a treatment for leprosy! They scarified the fellow, you say? Strung him up over a fire? That was *sinoo nganga* wood! Where did they find any, for the luff of Mike? Those neocapitalist swine in Moscow! They cost me Ilsa. She killed herself, you know, rather than give in to them! The empty Nembutal jar was under her body. Oh Gott, I would have understood! If the greedy pigs had only asked me I would have told them anything. *Sinoo nganga! Sinoo nganga!*' He pounded feebly on the reference book.

Hans gave me his son's address where he was going to rest up for a while, and I went and waited on the beach road to wave down the limousine service.

The long slab of black car approached within a few minutes, its bodywork dented and scraped along the doors and rear wing. A green window powered down, revealing a friendly gaunt face and haunted eyes.

'Sal, you even have your peaked cap on.'

'For forty-eight hunnerd dollars, you can have me in a party frock.'

I got in.

'Is that what I paid?'

We rode 99 across the central plain, past the air-force base, alongside Pearl Harbour, forking onto 70 to pass behind downtown Honolulu. Insulated by the status of humble working stiff, Sal had been allowed by Lau's men to pick up the limousine from the foot of the hill where unknown to them Mickey the ham was being cured. They'd told him he was being discharged on his own recognizance, cautioning against a possible Federal charge of trespass. I got out the wad and peeled him off ten bills for a lawyer if it happened, which I doubted – influential people would be closing ranks, not stirring up publicity.

We pulled in outside the off-beach Waikiki hotel I'd chosen randomly from Peppi's phone book. It resembled a cash register made of glass-ended rooms.

'Night's sleep recommended, rapido.'

I patted my fat pocket. 'About the bodywork – '

'Tip takes care of that. And skip the island first thing, okay?'

'After I find Peppi, yeah.'

Sal studied me.

173

'Cody, you seem to forget.'

'Huh?'

'Spray's loose. He snuck away when the goons rolled up.'

I shrugged off the thought of Spray. 'Reckon the guy's got other fish to fry. Thanks anyway, be talkin' t'ya.'

At reception, in breeze-dried shirt (a little crumpled and soiled), with wrung-out jacket hung casually low against my leg, cash and a whimsical name would do nicely, thank you. I crossed the clerk's palm handsomely, and ran to ground.

Kneeling at a bath running a cold showerhead over my neck for five minutes helped reduce the synapse trauma and prefrontal lobe pain. Two hours forty minutes flopped out on the time machine did some work on my molecular biology. I shaved with the courtesy disposable razor, and called the desk. There were no messages for Mr Kona C. Gale of Compton, California. There was a news slot available on the TV and I kept an eye on it while I fanned out the damp contents of my pockets to dry on the air conditioner grillework. What the news commissars served up was the usual batch of rehashed PR releases and managed leaks. The late Messrs Rayner and Lau might as well have been out tuna fishing with the Rotary. It figured. Tight little community, the Pacific Ocean.

The leg was stiff after sleep. I took it with me in the elevator down to the bar, a dim red-lighted affair haunted by private-looking people, with some not-so-private women. One Whit-bread's export ale went down swiftly, chased by a double Glenfiddich straight no ice. Another double Glenfiddich I savoured, feeling the effect melt into my wound and other areas.

For a while, comforting glimpses of a return to humdrum normality entertained me. My historical photographs had to be waiting at the Bishop museum and the state archives. They'd been due for pick-up at the end of my stay. There'd been that call from Doubleday's West Coast office on my machine at home. Mother would be wondering about the weekly letter home. And there was Laurie to remember, like I'd promised. Except I couldn't remember. She seemed to have gone. I finished a third whiskey browsing a menu which failed to inspire the huge potential appetite which was lurking somewhere. After ordering a steak rare, two beers and half a dozen apples from room service I went back to room 1212.

Eating upset me. Waiting made it worse. I lay on my back in a tremble. Lights on, lights off, radio music on/off, TV on/off, made no difference. Time lay on my chest like inquisitors' stones. Pent-up fear and insecurity started excreting all over my imagination. Peppi dying. Me in Folsom, punked and junked, property sequestrated. Hans felled by shock. Sal doing two-to-five back East. I ran through Lau being a hero and a patriot that I'd misjudged and helped to bring down. I ran through Pete Harman being a dangerous lunatic that I'd humoured and robbed. I thought how I could've saved Rayner.

A mugshot on the muted TV grabbed me. Wavy gypsy-king coiffure, a brass death's-head pendant on the left earlobe, face all halves: half-profile, half-pretty, half-tough, half-baked. It was a typical studio eight-by-ten, the type actors circulate. Station news, but nonetheless probably the biggest audience the face of Belkin Spray had ever surveyed. Grabbing the remote and pincering its sound control, I managed to catch the gist of the item: armed and dangerous, massive police hunt, first cold-blooded murder of lieutenant of detectives in Hawaii's history. Spray'd found stardom, with Petreen directing, I assumed.

A knock at the door rippled my digital switches. For a moment I cowered in disarray, cursing the way I'd stepped over Hedwig Maronek's automatic to dispose of Pete Harman's syringe.

Something tentative and vulnerable about the second knocking melted my fears and sent me on a binge of hope. Pain evaporated from my leg as I floated to the door and opened up.

It was a tall, elegant apricot-haired gentlewoman in a chic metropolitan two-piece suit made of silvery brushed cotton. Spruce in a cream blouse with a killer-whale brooch at the neck, she had high heels which with the short skirt made her legs look like porcelain. Her hair had been brushed to a blaze. All Peppi flowed back, mainly to my balls.

Then I took in the sickly pallor, the wilding eyes, the magnetic resonance of fear which snaked across the threshold into my diaphragm, causing me to snatch a silky arm reflexively and guide her into the room, shutting the door briskly behind us and latching it.

She shrank against the wall – tangibly warm and real, but ghostlike and barely able to speak. My grasping her shoulders and steadying her gaze seemed to help. She let it all out in a hurried mutter.

She'd been to draw up a will. She'd left anything she had to the Wellcome Foundation. The lawyer'd bought her dinner, talked up her problem.

I had to understand, she'd been around, run with show-business people, and things had been different then. Spray'd snatched her for a righteous reason, break her the news, try to talk her onto Rayner's project. She'd worried like hell, but couldn't figure out how to say it on the phone, or even write. It'd needed time.

No, she hadn't taken a test. The lawyer'd said there were groups she could join, thousands of people who could help her and she could help in return. Marriage was out of the question. Could I possibly comprehend?

The shock had been dreadful. Rayner'd given her a place to hide. Now life was like religion. Things of the flesh must be put away for ever. Everything had to be spiritual uplift. Her mother needed help on the Ganges. It was wrong to hope for a miracle, but even if it came, there could be no turning back. Fate had decreed her time on earth and such time must be lived on the path of wisdom divine.

'At least stay here the night,' I said.

Her eyes held mine, flickeringly.

'I'm so sorry, Cody.'

'I'm not. We'll charter something to Kauai in the morning. Hole up in Hans's shack on the beach. Fly out when the heat's off.'

'You don't understand,' she pleaded. 'I went home and found your note, and right while I was reading it, Belkin showed up. I got away from him, but he chased me here.'

In spite of myself, I suddenly let go of her.

'Spray? Where the heck is he?'

'He lost me. Maybe he's looking for this place.'

'He saw the note?'

'Ripped it out of my hand. Oh, Cody, I so wanted our dream to come true. We were all such bad girls once, now we know better, but it's too late. Suddenly I see oceans of suffering humanity, a future torn with war and drought and unpredictable hurricanes . . . '

She wandered on, so lost in it that I had to put thoughts of Spray aside, let her mouth work on its own and kiss her neck, holding her till she ran down.

The label had washed off the Femme de Rochas but she did like the fragrance.

'Maybe some . . . here, and how about . . . here,' I said.

'Get away.' Pushing the skirt down, but smiling, and she had garters on her stockings. It was time. We went and lay on the time machine.

As we were kissing, the telephone rang.

'Howdy Mr Tourist. Get your camera repaired?'

'I saw your portrait on the tube. You have a serious problem.'

'So've you. I snatched your sugar's maw from Rayner's place. Unless you hand over Harman's wad, she deep sixes off Molokai.'

I felt a grin spreading in the dark. Peppi murmured: 'Who is it?'

'What's the deal?' I said into the receiver.

'Get out to Peppi's place right away. There's a phone booth at the end of her road. Put four hunnerd thousand in cash on the phone and back your car off no less than fifty yards. Her mother gets escorted to the booth in full view, the escort takes the money out a the booth, she walks on. Geddit?'

'Listen, you shot a cop.'

'It's cooked.'

'There's still no way you'll buy an out.'

The voice took on a sneer.

'You're out a date, buddy. Hawaii's part a Asia now.'

'Uh-huh. Okay, you win. I have the money. I'll be right over.'

The receiver clicked and hummed. I pressed the bar.

Peppi's hand came to the phone and splayed warmly over mine. 'What's going on?'

'Just a moment.'

I got a number from information and dialed it.

'Quilley?'

'Yeah, who's this?'

'You wanna big climax to your career?'

'Cut the bullshit and talk.'

I talked. About Spray, and the venue of his next performance.

After I'd hung up, she let the clothes come away and me get at her juices, bathe in them, swallow them, wash them around with my own. If she was a dead duck, then my goose was cooking too and I told her I truly didn't mind.

Just when she started to coo and to hum and to kick up a womanly storm the cooling fans in the window bay kicked in and gusted a confetti of hundreds all over her glistening back and her bottom and her legs and we laughed.

'By the way,' I said. 'That call was about your mother. She's in town.'

'Gee, I wonder,' Peppi mused. 'You know Jung's theory of synchronicity? Something must've drawn her to the ceremony.'

The cable radio was playing low. Somebody far away was singing 'Rock On'.

We rocked on.

A NOTE ON THE AUTHOR

Rowland Morgan is a journalist and Press Officer for the Green Party. This is his first book.